THE SIGN OF THE CHRYSANTHEMUM

KATHERINE PATERSON

Illustrated by
PETER LANDA

HarperTrophy®
A Division of HarperCollinsPublishers

Library of Congress Cataloging-in-Publication Data
Paterson, Katherine.
    The sign of the chrysanthemum.

    Summary: A teenager comes to know himself through contacts
with social ills and political unrest while searching for his
father in Japan's capital, centuries ago.
    1. Japan—History—Heian period, 794-1185—Juvenile fiction.
[1. Japan—History—Heian period, 794-1185—Fiction]   I. Landa,
Peter, illus.   II. Title.
PZ7.P273Si   [Fic]   72-7553
ISBN 0-690-73625-8

    "A Harper Trophy book"
ISBN 0-06-440232-0 (pbk.)

Published in hardcover by HarperCollins Publishers.
First Harper Trophy edition, 1988.

Acknowledgments

With the exception of the ballad fragment on page 51, the poetry in this book has been taken from the literature that was known to Japanese living in the twelfth century. I should like to acknowledge the following sources and English translators:

Page 49. Yakamochi, died 785. Translation by Lois J. Erickson. *Songs From the Land of Dawn*. New York: Friendship Press, 1949, page 68. Copyright Friendship Press, New York, 1949. Used by permission.

Page 50. A fragment of a "Long Song" (*Naga Uta*) by Kakinomoto no Hitomaro (697–707), included in the *Manyoshu* collection. Translation by Kenneth Rexroth. *One Hundred Poems From the Japanese*. New York: New Directions Books, 1964, pages 113–114. All rights reserved. Reprinted by permission of New Directions Publishing Corporation.

Page 61. Anonymous poem, included in the *Kokinshu* collection, compiled 905. Translation by the author.

Page 124. Minomoto no Yorizane, included in the *Goshuishi* collection 1086. Translation by Donald Keene, *Anthology of Japanese Literature*. New York: Grove Press, 1955, page 95. Copyright 1955 by Grove Press, Inc. Reprinted by permission of Grove Press, Inc.

Page 124. Yamabe no Akahito (died 736). Translation by Kenneth Rexroth, *op. cit.*, page 3.

Pages 130–131. Excerpts from Isonokami no Yakatsugu (729–781), "The Small Hills." Translation by Donald Keene, *op. cit.*, pages 162–63. Copyright 1955 by Grove Press, Inc.

Among the sources used in the writing of this book, special thanks must be expressed to the authors of the following works:

Robert Newman, *Japanese—People of Three Treasures*. New York: Atheneum, 1964. Mr. Newman's description of the master swordmakers of Japan inspired the character Fukuji in this book.

Ivan Morris, *The World of the Shining Prince*. New York: Alfred A. Knopf, 1964. Mr. Morris' description of Kyoto in the Heian period proved invaluable, though any errors in authenticity are the present writer's own.

Eiji Yoshikawa, *The Heike Story*. Translation by Wooyenaka Uramatsu. Rutland, Vermont: Charles E. Tuttle Company, 1956. Published in Japan as *Shin Heike Monogatari*. The political and social life in Japan under Heike no Kiyomori was brought to life for me by Mr. Yoshikawa. I have also followed his lead in making Kiyomori a more sympathetic character than most historians allow.

I should also like to say "thank you" to Mary Jo Borreson, Elizabeth Branan, Bertha Bartol, Anne Womeldorf, Dr. and Mrs. Tomoyasu Tanaka, and my husband, John Paterson, for their help and to my children, Lin, John, Jr., David, and Mary, for their patience.

This book is for
John,
whose name means
God is gracious.

CONTENTS

THE SIGN OF THE
CHRYSANTHEMUM

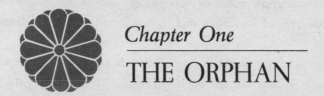

Chapter One
THE ORPHAN

Muna had not climbed the hill to the burial grounds since the last death among the serfs more than two years before, so that when he turned and saw the scene below, a thrill of pleasure went through his body. From a distance it was beautiful. The rice was all harvested now; and against the muted browns and greens of paddy and field, rice straw hung drying on the racks, golden under the late summer sun. On the bank of the shining river sprawled the roofs of the daimyo's manor, like a great, lazy cat stretched out for a summer nap. Across the fields the tiny thatched huts of the serfs tumbled upon one another like a litter of newborn kittens, drawing warmth and assurance from one another's bodies. Beyond field and hut and manor lay the ancient pine grove. And then the sea, its white waves crashing upon the rocky coast. And beyond the sea? By the gods, he would soon know. Soon, he promised himself, as he turned and began to dig his mother's grave.

His task complete, Muna returned to his hut to find old Sato's toothless wife washing the corpse. The boy knelt

1

down behind her on the dirt floor, his eyes downcast, his face drawn into a perfect mask of mourning.

"A kimono? Did the poor girl have a kimono for her burial?"

Muna got up wordlessly and fetched from the tiny chest the one decent garment his mother had ever owned. She had never worn it, of course. It had been saved for this day, so that no one would despise her poverty.

He settled himself once more behind the old woman, whose rough hands were dressing the dead woman with a kind of gentleness. He could read no expression in his mother's wasted face. "Her spirit will not be angry that I do not weep," he told himself. "Her life was only drudgery and grief, and death is her release. And mine." His heart beat faster. "And mine." For now, nothing held him here in Awa. He could make his way to the capital and begin his search.

"Beg pardon!" Muna turned to see Sato's ugly peasant face thrust through the doorway. "The priest has come." The serf's voice was drawn out in a solemn manner so unsuited to his comical features that Muna laughed silently, deep inside his belly.

"Poor Sato," he thought, "you and the old woman will have to plant the west field all alone now. Never, never again will I bend, ankle-deep in the mud like a water buffalo, until my back wants to scream out." But outwardly Muna was the grief-stricken orphan as he quietly rose to usher in the priest.

Muna had so little food to offer the few peasants who contributed their wails and prayers at the burial grounds that by nightfall the last one had shuffled home, leaving him alone in his hut to light the tapers and pray.

The flames pricked twin holes in the darkness, and for the first time the tiny hut seemed large with loneliness. Muna did not try to pray. He sat cross-legged before the makeshift altar, hugging his knees. She was gone. The only one who had cared for him. Until now, his mother and he had been like these two candles in a dark, unfriendly world. Tears started in his eyes.

"He was very big, your father." He remembered her breathless little girl's voice. "A fine samurai. Oh! And such a sword—taller than you, it stood."

In all her life, only the tall samurai was worth remembering. He had spent a few days on Awa, fathered her son, and never returned.

"It was rumored," she had said each time as though she were revealing a closely kept secret, "that he was on a special mission for his excellency, Heike no Kiyomori." Then, patting Muna's skinny knees, "He would be so proud of you. If only he knew."

"And he *will* know," Muna thought to himself as he wiped the back of his sleeve across his eyes and nose. "Little Mother," he whispered to the candle. "You think of me only as a child. You were frightened whenever I was out of your sight. But I am no longer a child. I must leave this miserable island and find a life worthy of a man. Until this day, I have let your fears hold me back from my dream. But watch me now without fear, for you will see your son come into his rightful inheritance. I am going to find my true name—the name of my father's people." His voice grew stronger. "I will be someone to be reckoned with in this world. No longer will men spit on me and call me Muna—the nameless one."

No. They will bow as I pass. They will prostrate themselves before me and beg favors of me. I shall wear a sword that will slay any man who dishonors my name—a great sword that will bring new glory to my noble father and to your spirit. But for a little while, I will have to leave your grave unattended while I accomplish these things. First, I must find my father. . . ."

"But how can you be sure that you are my son?" In his recurring daydream, the elegant warrior always looked down on him with a stern dignity that could not hide a wistful gentleness.

And Muna would look him straight in the eyes. "By the chrysanthemum."

At this, the great warrior's eyes would soften, and he would say, his voice choked with emotion, "My son, my son, the gods are good."

The boy was so lost in his dreamings that it was some moments before he became aware of another presence in the room. His mother's spirit? His lack of grief had offended her. Muna clapped his hand to his mouth to keep from crying out.

"Beg pardon, boy." To Muna's immense relief, he heard the graveled voice of Sato. "It is inexcusable to break into your mourning." The old peasant coughed importantly. "But a boat has come in. . . ."

A boat? Surely it was a sign from the gods.

". . . and the daimyo sends word that it must be unloaded at once."

Thank you, Little Mother. The boy bowed to the candles before he blew them out. "Go ahead, Sato. I shall follow directly."

The old man disappeared, murmuring phrases he thought appropriate for this solemn occasion.

As soon as Sato was well down the path, Muna jumped up. Hurriedly he took from a jar a few rice cakes he had hoarded from the funeral food, wrapped them in a kerchief, and stuffed them into his tunic.

He bound on a pair of straw sandals and tied a workman's cloth across his forehead. Then he ran down the narrow path between the huts, through the pine grove to the shore, the packet of cold rice cakes thudding against his chest with every step.

Chapter Two

KING OF THE PIRATES

There was a cloud across the moon, but retainers from the great house had brought torches, and in the pale light the serfs of Lord Yoshikuni, daimyo of Awa, moved in two ant-like lines up and down the gangplank. Sweat rolled in streams from the top of Muna's head and was absorbed by the cloth he had tied around his forehead. Like the others, he groaned a sort of singsong chant as he worked. Up the gangplank went much of the rice that they had labored so hard to produce; down the gangplank came the rolls of silk, the Chinese wines, and the other delicacies of court life in the capital which their daimyo desired in exchange.

Although he kept his head bent, Muna's eyes strained each time he boarded the boat and climbed down into the hold. He must find a hiding place that he could slip into without attracting notice.

"Boy! Stack the rice over there—against those other bales."

Muna shuffled over as though he were the dim-witted serf the overseer thought him to be. But when he got to the spot,

7

he put the bale down carefully, leaving just enough space for his own body between the two stacks.

"Hurry, stupid one!" The overseer called down into the hold. "*Ara!* Watch out! That's pottery. Don't drop it."

Muna nodded as stupidly as he could, climbed the ladder with the bale of pottery, and shuffled down the gangplank. He was delighted that his plan was working so well. Surely the gods were with him this night.

On each successive trip Muna watched the shipboard overseer for his chance. At last a sailor stopped to engage the man in agitated conversation. Muna quietly let down his load, quickly scrambled over the stack nearest the side of the hold, and slipped into his place between the rice bales.

Crouching there, he heard the last of the loading completed and the overseer's curt dismissal of the serfs. He even thought, through the noise of the sailors preparing to set sail, that he could hear the voice of old Sato calling his name.

"Muna? Muna?" How he hated his name. The daimyo had given it to him. The silly man had pretensions of being a Chinese scholar, and when Muna was born, he had thought it a huge joke to give a bastard serf a name which meant "no name."

But now the gangplank had been drawn in, and the boat was gently moving out from the dock into the Inland Sea.

At first Muna could feel nothing but the thrill of his adventure as he sat hunched over in the dark hold between the bales of rice. But as the small boat rocked out into the open sea and the heat in the hold became more intense, he began to feel something else in the pit of his belly. Hunger? He thought of the rice cakes, but he knew that they would have to last him for a journey of several days. It would be foolish to eat so soon.

Then he knew it was not hunger but something much more dreadful. Once when he was seven he had eaten a piece of old fish. . . . No, better not to think of his belly at all. He tried to conjure up the vision of his warrior father. He began with the long sword. To this he attached a great suit of armor and a magnificent horned helmet. Under that armor, there on the left shoulder, was the tiny chrysanthemum tattoo, the sign by which he would know that this noble samurai was indeed—

Suddenly the rude demands of his churning stomach overwhelmed every thought. He tried frantically to cling to the fading vision—to pray for the spirit of his mother—to sing a comic song Sato had once taught him. Useless, all useless.

He marveled to himself later that a boy who had put so little into his belly in an entire lifetime could be rid of so much in almost no time at all. He mopped up as best as he could with his headcloth and fell asleep, exhausted.

On deck, the ronin Takanobu helped himself generously to another bowl of rice.

"See here," the captain complained. "You've nearly eaten up our supplies by yourself. I should have known better than to take on a ronin to protect us. All the way over, not a pirate in sight. Just you, filling your great belly with my rice and guzzling down all my wine." He shook his head hopelessly.

Takanobu roared with laughter, letting bits of the precious rice fall out of his mouth. "Oh, come now, captain.

You're a lucky man to have me aboard. I could scare a fleet
of pirates just by snoring!" He laughed again at his own joke,
then with his chopsticks, delicately picked up each dropped
grain and popped it back into his mouth.

The captain watched, his lip stuck out in a pout. "How
came you to be a ronin, Takanobu? Did your lord catch you
stealing, or did the gods mercifully take him to Paradise
when they saw him being hounded to death by his own retainer?"

The ronin's eyebrows went up in mock surprise. "You're a
wit, captain. I have underestimated you. But, no, I became a
ronin by choice."

"Your lord's choice, no doubt."

"*Har, har, har!* A wit, a great wit." Takanobu finished off
is meal with another cup of the rapidly dwindling rice wine.
To you, my lord captain!" He pretended to salute his reluc-
ant host, then made his way a bit unsteadily across the deck,
nd climbed down into the hold. He was too tall to stand
pright below deck, but he seldom wanted to. He flung him-
elf down upon the mat that he used for a bed and prepared
o sleep.

"*Ummmm. Ummmm.*"

The renegade samurai sat bolt-upright now, hand on
word.

"*Ummmm.*"

The groaning came from the pile of rice bales in the stern.

Fully sober now, Takanobu crept across the floor and knel[against a bale, listening. Now along with the groaning h could hear steady breathing. Whoever the groaner was, h was asleep. There could be no question of that. Silently Ta kanobu moved back to the hold's opening and climbed th ladder. There, on deck, the night watch turned his lantern t see who approached.

"I need this lantern, sailor." The seaman opened hi mouth to protest, but they had all become so accustomed t the high-handedness of the warrior that he simply shrugge his shoulders as Takanobu disappeared into the hold onc more.

The bales were piled nearly to the low ceiling. Takanobu carefully pushed one aside so that he could spy on the myst rious groaner. It was a boy—from the looks of his clothe one of the serfs who had loaded the boat. He had stowe away.

Takanobu put his mouth to the crack. "Ahoy, there!" H said in a hoarse whisper.

The stowaway let out a stifled scream and sat up. The lan tern light was reflected in the boy's terror-stricken eyes.

"I am the king of the pirates. All aboard this boat are no my slaves." Takanobu gave a hideous low laugh.

Muna had no plan, no thought, except that he woul never be a pirate's slave. Not when his dream was so near t fulfillment. He put his head and shoulder against the stacl of rice bales and shoved with all his might.

Takanobu jumped out of the path of the tumbling bales holding the lantern away from his body. He had no desir for his little joke to end in the burning-up of the boa[

Meantime the boy was scrambling over the fallen bales, headed for the ladder.

Before he was halfway up, the warrior's hand held him fast by the back of his tunic. "Not so fast, puppy. If I put this lantern to your rear, you'll turn into an unhappy firefly."

"Let me go, you pirate dog!" Muna kicked backward furiously.

"Ouch!" The ronin cried out in respect. "Not a puppy—nor a firefly. You are a veritable donkey, my lad. Come now! Up the ladder you go." He released his hold, but before Muna could gain the top, Takanobu had drawn his long sword, and barely touching the boy's buttocks with it, followed him up the ladder and out onto the deck.

"Captain!" The captain and most of the crew came running. They had heard the noise of the falling bales and knew that the ronin was chasing more than rats.

"See what I've found you! Now admit it! I'm worth all the rice and wine I've cost you!"

"You said you were a pirate!" the boy cried out.

"So I am. So I am. In a manner of speaking."

The sailors roared with laughter. The boy's shoulders drooped.

Takanobu replaced his sword in its sheath and handed the lantern to one of the sailors. "Come, captain, a little rice for our hold rat."

"Rice! We're turning around and taking the little scalawag back this instant. Rice!" The captain spat on the deck. "You *are* a pirate, Takanobu."

"All right. Turn around, captain. You've a favorable wind. You'll lose at least a day, maybe more, and the season for typhoons is upon us. You'll be wooing the pirates. But turn around. You might lose face—taking a stowaway to the capital."

The captain made an angry noise in his throat. "You pirate. I'm holding you responsible for his fare."

"Of course, of course." Takanobu waved his hand grandly. "And now a bowl of rice, please, and a bit of dried fish."

But when they brought it, the boy found he could eat nothing, so Takanobu had to eat it for him. "To keep the captain from being upset," he explained.

Chapter Three
THE CAPITAL

There was a gentle wind from the south. The boat made its lazy way around the southern tip of Awaji Island and up its eastern coast, past the straits of Kii, which is the gateway to the great ocean. On board the sailors impatiently cursed the weakness of the wind, for it was nearly typhoon season and they were anxious to gain the safe mouth of the Kamo River, beyond the reach of sea storms as well as pirates.

But Muna knew no such impatience. His belly was at last making peace with the rocking of the boat, and he gazed contentedly out across the water toward the hazy mountain slope of the island in the distance.

"How's the belly?"

Muna gave a startled jump. The big warrior laughed, then hunched over the side of the boat until his head was at the boy's level.

"You haven't told me your name yet, puppy."

The boy stared down at the water. "They call me Muna."

"Muna? No name? What kind of a name is No Name?" Takanobu threw back his head and laughed. *"Har, har!"* The sound seemed to carry far across the shining waves.

Muna, his face burning, stood perfectly still, resisting the warrior's laughter as though it were a bodily assault. All the insults of a lifetime were bound up with the name "No Name." But now he was about to change it. He would find his father and the noble name that was rightfully his. He would show the serfs of Awa and this loutish ronin. . . .

The laughter stopped abruptly. "But who am I to laugh? If you are a boy with no name, you're no worse off than I." He thumped his chest. "I am a samurai with no lord—a ronin." Grinning, he gave the boy a friendly slap across the shoulders that nearly sent him flying overboard. "A ronin and a bastard. We make a good pair, eh?"

Muna turned and looked boldly at the man beside him. The wide tan face was framed above with a sloppily bound-up topknot and below with a beard that seemed to have grown without its owner's noticing or caring. The warrior's blue tunic and trousers were as faded and tattered as Muna's own. His feet were bare except for wooden clogs. But for the broad black sash that bound the long sword at his waist, no one would have taken him for a warrior.

Takanobu took a step backward, planted his feet apart, and placed his powerful hands on his hips. "There now, do you approve of me, puppy?"

Muna stuttered in his embarrassment. "I—I've never before seen a man who called himself a ronin."

"Is that worse than a boy who calls himself No Name?" He reached out, but this time Muna eluded the friendly slap that he feared might send him sprawling.

Suddenly the ship was alive with the shouting of sailors. "There ahead, puppy." Takanobu pointed. "The mouth of the Kamo. We'll be in Heiankyo by nightfall."

"Just where are you two pirates going?" the captain roared down to the landing stage where Takanobu had silently shepherded Muna when the old man's back was turned. "Takanobu! I want my fare, or the boy stays aboard!"

Muna looked up at the angry gestures of the captain and then at Takanobu's haughty face.

"The boy goes with me!" The ronin's roar could be heard above all the chanting and chatter of Rokuhara Port.

"Pay me!"

Takanobu threw both hands in the air in a gesture of transparent innocence. "Of course! By my honor!" Then through his teeth, he said to Muna: "Cross to the capital by Gojo Bridge. Go to Rashomon Gate." Muna hesitated. "Like the devil was at your back. Run!" He bowed elaborately toward the deck, covering the captain's view of the boy. "By the honor of this sword, I swear to you!"

"When?"

"Later!" bellowed the ronin. And he, too, showed his heels, leaving the captain red-faced and sputtering.

Muna was small for thirteen but easy on his feet. He picked his path across the bridge through the jostling crowd. It was dusk, and his slight form was soon lost among the peddlers and tradesmen on the bridge who had concluded their day's work on the docks or in Rokuhara itself.

"Clear the way! Clear the way!" Four retainers in silk brocade pushed back the crowd with their halberds, making way for a small ox-drawn carriage on the way to Rokuhara from Heiankyo. In Awa, not even the daimyo himself possessed such a cart. It was lacquered black, with flowers and butterflies engraved in gold leaf. The retainer's halberd was hard across his chest, or Muna might have dared reach out to

touch the cart. Perhaps his father owned such a carriage. For a moment he could imagine that behind the closed blinds sat a magnificent samurai going to visit Lord Kiyomori, chief of the Heike clan in his Rokuhara mansion. If his retainers wore silk, what must the man himself wear? And Muna bowed his head to the carriage—in case it carried his father or one of his relatives. Then it was gone, and he began once more to make his way across Gojo Bridge toward Heiankyo —the Capital of Eternal Peace—which lay on the other side.

For a short way Muna clung to the street that ran on the east side of the Kamo River; but it was growing dark, and he knew he must ask someone the way to the Rashomon Gate, if he were to find his way there that night. He turned eastward into the city at a broad thoroughfare, which in the warm late-summer evening jangled with the sound of boisterous music. There were many men in the street, and painted women leaned from the windows of the houses, smiling and calling down to them.

"Just a few coins!" An old woman sitting on the door stoop of one of the houses was calling out to the passersby. "You'll never miss the coins, and you'll never forget your evening!" She cackled as a man brushed past her into the house. Then she repeated her singsong invitation.

"Hey, you!" she called out. Muna had been standing before the house watching her, his mouth open in amazement. "You! Move along, boy! A face like yours is bad for business." She cackled again when some men lounging beside the building laughed at her joke. "A little green for the houses on Rokujo Avenue, wouldn't you say?" She asked them, indicating Muna with a point of her nose. They all laughed again.

Muna walked on quickly, his head down to hide his embarrassment. It was all too different from his expectations. Was this Heiankyo—the Capital of Eternal Peace? Where were the noble samurai with their quiet, graceful ladies? Where were the magnificent palaces and stately temples? Where, by the gods, was the Rashomon Gate? Or, at least, someone he could ask? Would everyone know him for a country fool before he even opened his mouth? Suppose he had lost Takanobu for good? The thought clutched at his belly like a sharp pain. He was alone in this terrible city. He would die, and his father would never know. He would die alone and nameless, and no one would care.

Little Mother, why did I leave your grave? Muna stum-

led through the darkened streets of the city. He passed a
emple and considered asking refuge for the night, but the
gates seemed high. With his ragged clothes and not even a
copper for the offering, he was ashamed lest the priest take
him for a common beggar.

Near the temple grounds, an old man was sweeping out a
iny shop. At first, Muna would have walked past, pretending
hat he knew where he was headed. But a smell of bean soup
rom the open doorway overcame his pride.

"Please forgive my rudeness, uncle. . . ." The man, hear-
ng the boy's rough country accent, looked up, and the si-
ence did not feel unkind, so it encouraged Muna to con-
inue. "I am only in the capital today, and I must meet an
cquaintance at the Rashomon Gate. . . ." Muna stopped.
His voice, which he had meant to sound manly and con-
ident, merely sounded pompous.

It betrayed his youth, for the man said, "Don't go there
fter dark, son. Rashomon is the pickpockets' paradise."

Muna was afraid if he spoke, he might cry. So with a laugh
hat ended more like a sob, he said, "But it doesn't matter. I
ave no money."

The old man shoved him into the house. "Akiko, we have
guest for supper," he called. Then he turned to Muna.
You must pay for your supper by telling my daughter and
e your story—where you have come from and how you
ade your journey to the capital."

The girl who appeared was surprisingly young; about his
wn age, Muna guessed. The old man, watching him,
ughed. "A pretty blossom for an old gnarled branch like
e, wouldn't you say?"

The boy hung his head, blushing as he did so. These cit
people could see into one's brain. "Don't worry. I'm no
offended. Now." His host indicated a cushion for Muna t
sit upon. "I am called Kawaki, the sandalmaker. We are hon
ored to have you in our humble shop. It is a rare treat for u
to entertain a guest from the provinces."

The warm food and the unexpected kindness of old K
waki and the girl, Akiko, filled Muna with a kind of happi
ness that he had never known before. But they were humbl
people, and he did not want to seem arrogant by bragging t
them about his samurai father. So in response to their que
tions, he said simply that he was an orphan who had come t
Heiankyo determined to seek his fortune. And to amus
them, he told them of his adventures on the voyage. Whe
he imitated Takanobu's ferocious manner—"I am the kin
of the pirates!"—Akiko, who had said nothing as she shyl
served his supper, became so caught up in the tale that sh

laughed aloud, forgetting to cover her mouth as she did so.

Muna was pleased. He began to tell the story especially for her. Her dark eyes sparkled with pleasure. To have a girl of his own age—indeed, any girl—admire him cheered his spirit in much the same way that the bean soup warmed his belly.

When he left the sandalmaker's shop early the next morning, Kawaki and Akiko walked part-way toward Rashomon Gate with him, begging him to come to see them again. He promised to do so, swearing to himself that he would reward them when he came into his inheritance.

How beautiful the capital seemed to Muna that morning, with the sun setting the clouds above the eastern hills afire. A pair of crows called to each other from neighboring roofs like a pair of old gossips. Muna wanted to laugh for joy. He broke into a little trot, taking deep gulps of the cool morning air as he ran.

Then he slowed to a walk, for out of the morning haze ahead he could see the outlines of the great gate. As he neared it, he realized that the gray forms at the base of the columns were human. They were the beggars who knew no other home.

Muna had seated himself on the steps of the gate to wait for the ronin when he heard a familiar sound. It was a healthy snore.

"Takanobu!" the boy shouted with delight. He ran to the sleeping body and shook it. "It's me, Muna. I found my way at last."

"Praise the devil!" snorted the ronin and rolled over to sleep again.

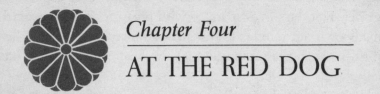

Chapter Four

AT THE RED DOG

While he waited for the snoring ronin to rouse himself, Muna stared in amazement at the scene, which as the morning grew older, came to life before the steps of Rashomon Gate. Fanning out on either side were row upon row of tiny stalls where if one had a little money, one could buy fish, cheap cloth, sandals, even amusement, for there were itinerant musicians to be seen, and under a tree three girls were dancing to the delight of a small crowd.

Peddlers passed by, bent under loaded frames, hawking clogs and good-luck charms, crickets in tiny bamboo cages. A noodle vendor, his brazier on one end of a bamboo pole and bowls of foodstuffs on the other, called out to the crowd. The smell of noodles bubbling in a meat broth assailed Muna's nose. Had he not eaten with the sandalmaker and his daughter, he would have perished. Even so, he found that he was hungry again.

The merchants were poorly clad, and their merchandise for the most part was inferior. But to Muna, who had known only the destitute life of a serf, they seemed quite grand. It was the others—the strange little creatures who seemed to live on the portico of the gate—who horrified the boy. They all looked alike, sharp little birdlike faces, dull eyes peering out from under filthy, matted hair. Rags, instead of clothes, hung from their bent frames.

One such creature was watching a woman roasting meat on spits over a charcoal brazier. The woman turned to speak to a customer who seemed to be complaining about the spit of meat he had just bought. The man smelled the meat elaborately, then stuck it under the woman's nose. Both of them gestured angrily. At last the man hurled the spit away. The elderly little creature who had been watching swooped down

upon it and snatched it up almost before it touched the ground. He darted toward the portico, but two younger beggars blocked his way. There was a scuffle in which the two others soon prevailed, snatching away the older man's prize. He screamed a curse on them and then, suddenly aged again, hobbled up the steps past Muna to a dark corner of the portico where he could nurse his disappointment.

The boy turned his face away. He was sickened by the whole scene, and he despised the creature whose wretchedness caused this discomfort. With relief he saw that Takanobu was waking up. Now they would soon be off to see the grand sights of the capital of which he had often dreamed.

"I don't suppose you have a copper on you," Takanobu asked as he washed his face at the public well located near the gate. Muna, squatting beside him, shook his head.

"My usual luck," the ronin shrugged. He stood up, wiping his face with the tail of his tunic. "So I borrowed a bit of luck from our friend the captain." He drew something from the fold of his garment which flashed in the sunlight. "First, I must find old Plum Face."

For a moment the boy failed to understand fully. Something was wrong, terribly wrong. The feeling buzzed about in his head like a huge wasp. Then it lit: *Takanobu had stolen something from the ship*. The samurai was a thief.

In Awa, Muna had seen a thief once, a serf, who had stolen a chicken from the daimyo's flock. The man's hands had been cut off, and his hut burned to the ground. The other serfs had thrown rocks as the thief ran, wounded and howling, into the hills.

Stunned with horror now, Muna followed this happy, joking thief through the marketplace.

Plum Face proved to be a peddler. He got his name, no doubt, from the large purple birthmark that marred the left half of his face. Muna found it hard to look into the man's eyes.

"Come now, Plum Face," Takanobu was arguing. "You know it's worth more than that. It's solid silver. Feel it."

"Who'd you steal it from?" The peddler's voice was harsh, but he took the object.

"Steal?" Takanobu asked ingenuously. "A family heir-loom—by my honor."

"*Ffftt.*" The peddler spat from the side of his crooked mouth. Then he turned the small silver Buddha over in his hands. Muna stared at his feet as Takanobu shifted about impatiently. Finally Plum Face drew a few silver coins from a purse at his belt. Takanobu stuck out his big hand and quickly closed his fingers over the money.

"Until next time, ronin," replied the humorless voice.

Takanobu started down Suzaku Oji, the broad willow-lined avenue that led from Rashomon Gate to the Imperial Palace with Muna, at his heels, skipping to keep up with his companion's long strides. As he walked, Takanobu tied the peddler's coins in a kerchief and shoved them into his tunic. So there was to be no punishment for the ronin's crime. The city was a strange place indeed. At Rokujo Avenue they turned west. Muna recognized it, his heart thumping, as the boisterous street where he had made a fool of himself the night before. He prayed no one would recognize him. At noon the street was a pleasant, bustling place, but the houses with the many latticed windows seemed to sneer down at him as he passed.

Takanobu turned abruptly into a doorway. "Welcome to

the Red Dog," he said over his shoulder as he pushed his way past the curtain which hung over the entrance.

The tiny room was nearly filled with men, eating and drinking noisily. Most of them were as ragged as the ronin and Muna himself. A few looked up to smile and nod.

"Ah, welcome home, Takanobu. It has been a long time," a young waitress called out.

"Yah. It's good to be home, Reiko." Takanobu patted the girl's cheek. "How's your beautiful mistress?"

A fat woman stuck her face through the doorway at the back. "No credit!"

Takanobu threw both hands in the air. "You never trust me, auntie!"

He motioned to Muna to sit down and ordered noodles for them both and rice wine for himself. The fat woman stood over them, glowering. With elaborate gestures, Takanobu withdrew the kerchief from his tunic, untied the corner, and pressed one of the silver coins into the woman's hand. She looked at the coin as though she doubted its validity. Then with a shrug and a snort, she produced the change in copper coins from the purse at her waist and retired once more to the kitchen.

Two men wearing swords joined Takanobu and Muna at their low table. "Koishi, Ogasa—my friend Muna, little No Name."

Muna bowed and tried to hide his blush. The men nodded toward him without interest.

"Now tell me, Koishi," said Takanobu, "from which direction is the wind strongest these days?"

"From the west," replied the shorter of the two men.

"So?" Takanobu's eyebrow went up.

"Without doubt," Ogasa said. "But winds have been known to change, eh?" Takanobu smiled. Muna was afraid to break into this peculiar conversation, but he could make nothing of what the men were saying. He was all the more confused then when Takanobu said, "I thought the boy might get a job in the stables. A good place to sniff the wind, don't you agree?"

The men laughed and began to settle Muna's future among themselves, without consulting him. It was decided that Ogasa should take Muna to the Imperial stables as soon as they finished eating, for the sooner he was at work the better.

"And besides," said Takanobu, "I have these coins to get rid of along Rokujo Avenue tonight. No place for a beardless boy, now is it?"

The others slapped their knees and laughingly agreed.

It seemed strange, even to a country boy like Muna, that these ragged ronin should have influence in the Imperial stables. As it turned out, Ogasa knew a bean-cake vendor who knew a tavern maid who knew one of the grooms at the stables. The groom agreed to take the boy on in repayment for a modest bribe. Thus by afternoon Muna had become one of the boys who worked and lived in the stables of the Imperial Guards.

The stableboys were not trusted to groom the valuable war-horses of the guardsmen. They cleaned the stalls and carried feed for the animals and served the grooms and soldiers assigned to the stables. The hours were long and the work hard, but at the beginning Muna did not complain, for he

was warmer and better fed than he had ever been in Awa. In addition, there was the glamour of the scene to feed upon— the beautiful horses and magnificent samurai, both Genji and Heike, who rode them. Why, one of them might be his own father! But the glamour dimmed as Muna realized that the stable captain never allowed the boys to speak to the guardsmen. "It is as though we were outcasts," Muna grumbled to himself.

The incident between Takanobu and Plum Face had stuck in the boy's throat like a bone. But now, as he compared the ronin to the unapproachable Imperial guardsmen, it was a kind of comfort that the ronin, at least, did not despise him—in fact, had saved his hide from the ship's cap-

tain. And somehow morality in the capital seemed written in a language the boy did not yet understand. In Awa the poor lived forever under the heel of the daimyo, nor did it ever occur to them they might do otherwise. But here was Takanobu—one of the luckless of the world by his own admission—who felt no obligation to live out his life under anyone's foot. If one is luckless, the ronin seemed to reason, he should make his own luck—or borrow it, or steal it. Takanobu did the last with such a flourish that even his victims could not wholly despise him. And Muna, whom he had befriended, fell more and more under the ronin's roguish charm. He began to tie his hair up on his head in the untidy version of a samurai topknot that Takanobu affected.

Muna's voice was changing pitch, so there was little to be done with it, but he did practice in private Takanobu's merry obscenities and irreverent manner of address.

Indeed, as his preoccupation with the ronin grew, the vision of his father dimmed. In his mind he justified the fact that he was not searching for his father by telling himself that he had to learn more about the capital, make friends with influential persons, before he could pursue his search. Besides, didn't he owe something to the man who had saved him from the ship captain's wrath and helped him get work in the city?

Though it was never agreed upon in so many words, Muna would take the few coppers he earned each week and give them to Takanobu, who had not yet managed to find himself a job. They always met in the Red Dog. Usually either Koishi or Ogasa would join them. Invariably the men would press Muna for gossip he had picked up from the soldiers. He began to enjoy filling their hungry ears with the tales he heard and would make a special effort to hang about the soldiers to learn extra tidbits for his weekly audience.

"Ah, this week the Genji warriors are angrier than ever," he reported one night late in November.

"So?" said Takanobu, and all three men leaned closer to Muna.

Of course the boy did not know what the Genji members of the Imperial Guards were thinking. He got no closer to these exalted figures than their horses' feed troughs, but he knew what the stable soldiers and the grooms were saying. This he reported with the air of one who had eavesdropped upon state secrets. "His Majesty has given Lord Kiyomori another large estate. He heaps more and more honors now on the Heike." He paused, concentrating on his teacup. "I fear the Genji are very jealous for their clan." The men smiled at each other. "As well they might be," continued Muna. "Lord Kiyomori of the Heike is the greatest samurai in Japan."

There was a silence. Ogasa cleared his throat noisily.

"I didn't know you were such a great admirer of the Heike, puppy." Takanobu slouched on an elbow and stretched his long legs out on the mat floor.

"Yes." Muna's eyes were shining. "I saw him once at the stables. He is not very tall, you know, but very powerful. He looked toward me, and I began to shake all over." The men laughed. "I guess I never told you." Muna's voice was as casual as he could make it. "My father is a Heike warrior."

"Oh?" Takanobu poured himself more wine. "How do you know?"

"Why, my mother told me." All three men were looking at him, but he could not read what their expressions meant. He wished at once that he had not told them. They would think him a silly braggart.

As the weeks went by, it became apparent to Muna that the three men had cooled toward him. Each week he stored up more to tell them, but they seemed less interested than before. Twice when he went to the Red Dog, none of them appeared; and he had to leave his money with the girl Reiko and trust her to get it to Takanobu. He repented often that he had spoken of his father. He felt sure that he had offended the ragged ronin who had been such a friend to him.

It was a cold winter. The rivalry between the warriors of

the Genji and Heike clans increased. For as the soldiers spent the long winter evenings huddled around their tiny charcoal burners, they talked. And in their idle talk, they stumbled upon grievances they had not realized themselves.

The stableboys were disgruntled, too, for the captain had ordered a thorough scrubdown of the stables in preparation for the New Year according to the Chinese calendar. The day before New Year's Eve was Muna's fourteenth birthday, but he hardly remembered it. His hands were raw and cracked from the icy scrub water, and he was exhausted from the extra work. He wanted nothing more than a long sleep under his quilt in the corner of the stable, but he knew Takanobu might be waiting, and he did not want to disappoint him.

"Welcome home, Muna!" Takanobu waved to Muna as he entered the Red Dog. All three men were there, and they greeted him warmly. "Reiko, some warm wine for the boy. See how cold he is!" Takanobu called out.

So they had forgiven him his stupid bragging, or perhaps he had only imagined their coldness. Muna smiled gratefully as Takanobu poured the steaming wine into his cup. Always before they had ordered tea for him. He sipped the white liquid and let it warm him. He was so cold and tired.

"Hey—don't go to sleep! We need you, puppy."

Muna straightened and forced open his eyes.

"To the Rashomon Gate," Takanobu was saying. "I'd go by myself, but the foolish Plum Face is angry and might refuse to speak to me at all."

"Terrible man when he's angry." Koishi twisted one side of his mouth in a clumsy imitation of Plum Face's leer.

"Wicked fellow," agreed Ogasa, elaborately blowing his nose.

Muna was still drowsy when he stumbled out of the Red Dog, clutching the folded note that Takanobu had given him to take to Plum Face. But the freezing drizzle soon pierced his thin tunic and made him uncomfortably alert.

Despite the weather and the hour, the streets were crowded. Everyone was busy preparing for the New Year. The creatures who lived in the shadow of Rashomon Gate were also bustling about. Some were washing their wretched garments in the icy water from the public well, ludicrous figures clad only in loincloths and goose bumps. The stalls of Thieves' Market were being scrubbed down, just as the Imperial stables had been earlier in the day. Even to these, the scum of the capital, the New Year held out a magical hope for something better than they had ever known.

Muna moved through the throng looking for Plum Face. He had never gotten over his shyness with city people, especially these. Their poverty was not strange to him, but everything else about them was. He hesitated to speak, for he hated to be laughed at by such as these. But when he was sure that Plum Face was not in sight, he approached one of the communal bonfires. For a few moments he squatted quietly, warming his hands. Out of the corner of his eye, he studied the man beside him. The face was old and pitted with smallpox scars. Others in the circle were shouting and laughing across the fire, but the old one was staring quietly into the flames. Muna leaned closer and said into the old man's ear: "Excuse me, grandfather, but have you seen Plum Face the peddler tonight?"

The old man turned slowly and looked into Muna's face. His dull eyes were red-rimmed from the smoke. "He is dead, boy. Nearly two months now. But if you have something you must sell, old Nishiwa in the Thieves' Market. . . ."

Dead? Plum Face dead? And for two months? Why hadn't Takanobu heard by now? He murmured an apology to the old beggar and started back toward the Red Dog.

In his mind he went over the conversation he had had earlier with the three ronin. There had been something peculiar, something he could not quite understand, about their behavior. Perhaps it was one of Takanobu's jokes.

That was it. He could see the men now, back in the Red Dog, warm from their wine, laughing at him for going out into the freezing night like a stupid, trusting old dog. Muna unfolded the note. It was too dark to see the writing, which he could not have read even if he could have seen it. He crumpled the paper and let it fall to the street. The more he thought of the ronin and his friends, warm and merry from their wine, their raucous voices calling out his name in derision, the more irritated he became. He had nearly decided to return directly to the stables and leave them to their laughter when something in the air caught his attention.

Above the rooftops there was a light. He began to run toward it. Now he could smell the smoke and hear the sounds that came from the direction of the west and Rokujo Avenue. Like pigs at the slaughtering. The gods have mercy! Takanobu and the others would be dead-drunk by now. All his irritation vanished as he ran. Takanobu was his friend.

He pushed through the crowd that clogged the entrance to the avenue. In the confusion of soldiers trying to put out the fire and the painted ladies and their customers who were seeking to escape, no one tried to stop a skinny boy dodging through the confusion straight into the heart of the blackest smoke.

He could hardly breathe, but he forced his body through the searing heat until he came to where the Red Dog had stood. "Takanobu! Takanobu!" the boy cried out, choked by the smoke and the sight before him. For the insatiable dragon had already engorged the flimsy wooden structure and had gone on, belching flames, to satisfy its appetite elsewhere.

"If only I hadn't left him!" the boy cried, cursing himself as he stumbled toward the river at the end of the avenue. "I should have known he was drunk. I should have known he was teasing again."

And then Muna collapsed.

Chapter Five
FUKUJI

On New Year's Eve, the freezing rain turned to a wet snow. Fukuji, the swordsmith, stood in his back doorway and watched the flakes drift into the courtyard, melting as they hit the cobblestones. He would be fifty in the year ahead. By the current reckoning he was an old man, but he neither looked nor felt old. For many years he had kept both spirit and flesh so strictly disciplined that now his short, powerful body conveyed the vitality and alertness of a great buck deer.

But as he watched the fragile flakes melt on the stones, he felt in his heart the pain of a man who has known many years and many lives that began in brightness only to fall and disappear. Suddenly he was homesick for snow—snow such as fell in his native province. He longed for snow to cover the earth in gleaming quiet, to give his squalid, fractious city a day of stillness at the New Year.

This was the first New Year since his wife had died twenty-five years before that Fukuji had had company for the holiday. A strange guest, to be sure. More like a sparrow fallen from its nest. Last night the swordsmith had gone to the fire when the alarm was called, and he had stumbled over a limp form in the street. He had picked up the boy and carried him home, not knowing if he was alive or dead.

He could hear the rattled breathing of the boy from within the house. Fukuji crossed the stone floor of the kitchen and stepped up into the house. The boy lay in the inner room. Fukuji had laid him on his own pallet and covered him with quilts. The boy was not badly burned, but he had breathed in the foul smoke and poisoned his lungs. Now he burned with fever. Fukuji wiped the young face. He went down into the kitchen and rinsed the rag in cold water from the well, wrung it out, and replaced it on the boy's forehead. The child opened glazed eyes, but Fukuji could not tell whether he was conscious or not.

He had sent a neighbor's boy to fetch a doctor earlier, but many had been injured the night before in the fire, and there was no doctor free to come to the shop. So Fukuji nursed the boy as best he could. He washed the thin body with well water in a battle with the fever that seemed to grow more intense by the hour. Each tortured breath the boy took cut through Fukuji's own chest like a jagged knife.

"The snow falls and disappears," he thought without hope.

But he fought on through the night, doing the only thing he knew to do—washing the boy's burning trunk and limbs with the icy water.

Just before dawn, the fever broke. Sweat poured from the boy's body, soaking the pallet. Fukuji piled every quilt he owned on the small bony frame, then stretched himself out on the bare mat floor and fell asleep.

When he looked out the next morning, the courtyard was white with a thin covering of snow.

In the streets of the capital, children frolicked in the snow. They divided themselves into rival teams of Heike and Genji and bombarded each other with snowballs. But in his villa at Rokuhara, General Kiyomori of the Heike clan was in no mood for games.

"The capital is seething with rumors, sir." Tada, his retainer, was speaking. The two men were sitting cross-legged on the mat floor, sipping warmed rice wine. The general's face was set in grim lines as he listened to his retainer's account of the New Year's disturbances in the capital.

"Is there any evidence that General Yoshitomo is behind the troubles?" Yoshitomo was chief of the Genji clan and thus Kiyomori's prime rival for power.

The retainer shook his head. "No one knows. People will say anything. It is even said in some quarters"—the warrior glanced sidelong at his lord—"that the fire on Rokujo Avenue was set at *your* command."

"*Pfoo.*" Kiyomori made a sound of disgust at this absurd rumor. "And what is being said in court?"

"On the surface, nothing. Presumably everyone is so involved in the New Year's feasting that they've hardly noticed the fires and the street-squabbling among the soldiers. But you may be sure that those wine-reddened noses are sniffing the wind."

"And the young Emperor?"

"I think Councilor Shinzei can assure him of your loyalty."

"Hmmm, I wonder. There are many Genji mouths pouting about the court these days."

"Then will you take some action?"

"Ah, Tada, I am a soldier a bit weary with soldiering. We have had scarcely two years of peace. I need time to see to my own affairs." He took a long sip of the wine and sighed. "I have not yet made a pilgrimage in honor of my father's death—and he has been dead nearly six years. If war comes, it comes, and I will fight. But I will not blow on the embers. The fire that burns the city may destroy Rokuhara as well."

The fire that had burned in Muna's body died slowly. The raging visions of his delirium focused into one cold line.

Takanobu is dead.

His eyes were slower in focusing on his unknown surroundings, but his brain beat out the one thing it remembered: *Takanobu is dead. Takanobu is dead.*

In Awa there was a grove of pines along the shore. The wind off the sea had twisted the ancient trunks and limbs, so that they bent grotesquely against the strength of it, their roots like gnarled fingers holding tenaciously to the rocks.

There was one tree—Muna must have been very young when he discovered it—one tree that stretched out a giant arm across the rocks. As long as he could remember, Muna had run to it and climbed into the lap that the great limb made at the trunk. It was his place for sorrow and anger and dreams. He could sit there quite hidden, for the upper limbs bowed over the large lower one, making a tent with their profusion of green needles.

When the other peasants called him "Muna, the no name," and taunted him as a nothing that even such as they could despise, Muna would flee to the tree and stay for

hours huddled against the trunk. He would listen to the waves roar in and break on the rocky shore, and harden his ears against the piteous cry of his mother. "Chi Chan! Chi Chan!" She never called him Muna, but "Little One," a baby name he both liked and resented. "Chi Chan! Chi Chan!"

The waves roared in. *Takanobu is dead. Slap the unfeeling rocks. Takanobu is dead. Crash the cruel rocks.* In his comforting green haven the smell of resin and needles tickled his nose.

His nose. He began to be aware that the lining of his nose and throat were burning with each breath. The fire on Rokujo Avenue. He remembered now the smoke and the choking despair. But how had he come here—to this strange haven between a pallet and warm quilts? He fingered the padded cover. It was a coarse, cheaply dyed material, but to Muna it seemed very grand. He propped himself up on one elbow. Before him was a wall of shutters, which to judge by the sounds from the other side, opened directly onto the street. So he was in a shop of some sort.

To his left, sliding paper doors were pushed back revealing a room of equal size where he could see a low table and beyond, a step or two lower down, the kitchen.

But when he turned to look to his right, he saw with a thrill of wonder what sort of shop it was, for the right wall was hung with swords. Some of the long swords hung in scabbards, richly ornamented with jeweled birds and flowers. But several of the weapons were unsheathed, their long curved blades catching the dim winter light from the kitchen doorway.

To Muna the swords seemed to be almost living creatures as he watched them, the light dancing over the varying surfaces of the gleaming blades. His father would own a sword like one of these.

His father. In the months since he had come to the capital, the dream of the brightly armored samurai had grown dimmer rather than brighter. Strange. At first as he worked in the stables, he had sought out a Heike retainer of one of the guardsmen and tried in his shy country way to ask him of his father. But he stuttered and blushed as he heard himself asking if the soldier might know a high-ranked Heike who had served General Kiyomori fourteen years ago in Awa. Even as he framed the question, he became aware of its absurdity. The stable master interrupted then with one of his kicks, sending Muna back to work. The boy was almost grateful to be spared the look of ridicule on the Heike retainer's face.

Muna had continued to listen to the conversations at the stables. But more and more, he realized, he had listened for stories to tell Takanobu and not for clues to his father's identity.

But a swordmaker's shop! Once again the boy felt that the gods had interfered. Takanobu had been taken so that he might begin to search in earnest for his father. And what better place to begin than in a swordmaker's shop? A swordmaker like this one would know all the prominent samurai in the capital. "I must make him like me," Muna thought. "I must make him want me to stay on with him." Muna breathed a prayer for help to the spirit of his mother—and for good measure, a prayer to the spirit of Takanobu, though he had private reservations as to the ronin's standing on the other side.

Then he began to cough, so he lay back between the warm bedding. Later there would be plenty of time to investigate the house.

"A New Year has dawned. I wish you happiness."

At the traditional greeting, Muna turned with a start. A man, surely the swordsmith himself, knelt beside the quilt.

"A New Year has dawned," Muna replied in a strange, hoarse voice. "This year, again, I beg your kindness."

"Rest quietly," the man said. "Don't try to talk. Here." He propped a quilt behind Muna's head. "See if you can drink some New Year's soup with me. I beat out the rice dumplings on the anvil. That should make them especially lucky, eh?"

Something warned Muna that the swordsmith was joking, and he ventured a smile. The man grinned in reply. "He isn't going to be so hard to please," thought Muna. The hot, sugared soup hurt his raw throat, but Muna drank it down manfully. Everything was going to be all right. The swordsmith liked him already.

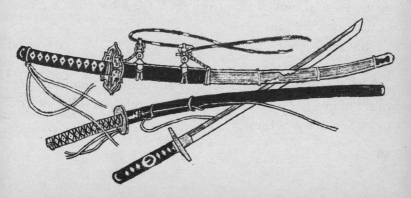

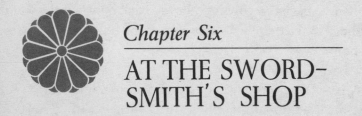

Chapter Six

AT THE SWORD-SMITH'S SHOP

By the time the plum tree in the courtyard bloomed, Muna had completely thrown off the lung sickness, and though it was still quite cold outside, he insisted to his host that he was well enough to take on his full share of the chores. Muna wanted the swordsmith to see how much help he could be, but his eagerness, which tended to make him careless and hasty, ran counter to Fukuji's precise and methodical system of life.

"Sir, the rice is prepared," Muna had called the first morning at the closed forge door, bowing nervously.

"Ready, now?" There was a clank as the swordsmith put down his hammer and came to the door of the forge. He opened it and looked up at the sky. "It's more than an hour until noon," he said.

"But in an hour," said the boy miserably, "the rice will be cold."

The swordsmith sighed. "Yes, well, perhaps tomorrow you could remember to look at the sky before you put the rice on to boil, don't you think?"

He started for the house with the chastened Muna trailing him. In the center of the courtyard Fukuji stopped and looked around. "You haven't swept the yard yet?"

Muna hung his head, but inside he was boiling with humiliation. "I was worried about the rice, and I forgot."

"Yes, well—shall we eat first? Then perhaps tomorrow. . . ."

But on each succeeding tomorrow, Muna either collided headlong with the swordsmith's orderly plan for the day or missed it altogether. The rebuke was always the same: "Yes, well, perhaps another time you might. . . ." Muna would have preferred the sharp blows of the overseer under whom he had worked in Awa. One could despise the overseer, growing fat on the serfs' labor, but who could despise a man like Fukuji?

There was a purity in the way the swordsmith devoted himself to every task. He never demanded of Muna nearly what he demanded of himself. From the kitchen door Muna would marvel as he watched him cross the courtyard to the forge. Fukuji wore a white garment, such as a priest might wear, when he was forging a new blade. To the boy he looked like a god, his grizzled hair and beard cropped close to his head. And though he always closed the door of the forge behind him, Muna liked to imagine him there, his powerful arm moving in a perfect rhythmic motion as he brought the great hammer down *Clang! Clang! Clang!* forcing the stubborn metal into obedience to his will.

The boy knew without words that he was not to enter the forge, for it was like the holy place in a shrine that no one could enter but the priest. Fukuji had no apprentice. He had

told Muna that there were few boys in the capital whom he would consider taking on, and the best of these had gone to join one of the rival clans of Genji or Heike and had been swallowed up in the insurrection against Emperor Go-Shira Kawa two years before. But the swordsmith was accustomed to living and working alone, and did not mourn that there was no one to inherit the secrets of his craft. The swords would remain, of that he was sure. They were his sons, his disciples, and his epitaph. To them he devoted his life.

In those first months Muna found the daily exposure of his inadequacies hard to bear. He might have left the sword-smith if it had not been for music. In the evenings Fukuji would go to the storehouse beside the forge and fetch his six-stringed zither; and in the cold, clear nights of early spring the two of them would sit in the courtyard, the boy entranced while the swordsmith plucked his instrument and sang melancholy ballads of his native province and classical poems that he himself had set to music.

From his massive body Fukuji's voice came out surprisingly clear and boyish. And the beauty of it made Muna hug his knees to keep from shaking.

> Night:
> And a doorway left ajar
> In the white moonbeams;
> For you promised your spirit would
> come to me, Love,

The calloused hands caressed a mournful sighing chord from the strings.

> In my dreams!

And then quickly he would turn to a comic song of the peddlers on the Gojo Bridge, his broad fingers dancing gleefully across the strings.

The swordsmith never spoke of his wife, but one night he sang Hitomaro's "Song of Mount Hagai," which tells of the poet's searching the mountain for the spirit of his dead wife.

> I struggle over the ridges
> And climb to the summit.
> I know all the time
> That I shall never see her,
> Not even so much as a faint quiver in
>   the air.
> All my longing, all my love
> Will never make any difference.

And pain flashed so brightly through the crystal voice that Muna almost forgave him for being a god and perfect.

There were ballads of gallantry and war—though these were not necessarily the same. For there was one song of the insurrection two years before that made Muna understand for the first time the depth of hatred between the two clans in their struggle for power over the nation. It told of Yoshitomo of the Genji, who as a member of the Imperial Guards felt obliged to side with Kiyomori of the Heike when the rest of his own Genji clan joined in a revolt against the Emperor. The white banner of the Genji waved beside the red banner of the Heike as together they went out against Yoshitomo's father and brothers. And in the end Yoshitomo had been forced by his allies to order the death of his father.

His father had been a traitor to the Emperor, and traitors

must die. Yoshitomo did not deny this. He had his father and his kinsmen executed so that there could be no whispers about his own loyalty. And yet, as he watched them die, he could not stifle within his breast a fierce hatred against the Heike clan—united, strong, arrogant in victory, while most of the warriors of his own clan must die in disgrace, their flesh a feast for carrion crows.

> *And my blood cries out to you, my son,*
> *The white banner is stained with scarlet.*
> *Turn and see, turn and see, the mighty*
> *   house brought low.*

When he finished the ballad, Fukuji shook his head. "Pride, pride, pride. It will slay us all in the end."

"Whose pride, Fukuji?" Muna was bold enough to ask because he needed to know. He had been caught in the rivalry at the stables and torn by his own loyalty to his Heike father and to Takanobu whom he suspected of sympathy with the Genji. "Is it the pride of Heike or Genji that will slay us?"

"Both," the man said. "Or"—he rose to put away the zither—"or perhaps neither. Perhaps a man is never truly destroyed except by his own hand."

So Muna stayed on at the swordsmith's shop, and as the days turned warmer, he became more proficient in the chores that Fukuji assigned to him. The more proficient he grew, the more he came to despise the tasks that once had seemed so formidable. They were, after all, mere woman's work. At the next New Year he would be fifteen, the age when boys became recognized as men, and before then he must find his father and begin a life more suited to his position. But how could he find his father? Should he speak to Fukuji about him?

"Excuse me," a voice called from the entryway of the shop, interrupting his self-questioning one afternoon late in March.

Muna hastened up from the kitchen to greet the caller. His heart pounded to see the tall Heike guardsman standing in the entryway. He knew their style of dress from his life in the stables.

He crouched, bowing his head to the mat. "Welcome, sir. If you will come up and be seated, I will call my master." He longed to speak to the samurai himself. If he could speak to the man, he might know instinctively if he had met his father.

He hesitated, waiting as the samurai seated himself on one of the cushions beside the low table. But when the magnificent warrior turned toward him, Muna lost his nerve. He gave a hasty bow and ran out to fetch the swordsmith.

As the two men sipped tea and talked in the front of the house, Muna pretended to be busy in the kitchen, listening intently for some clue of voice or manner that might reveal the tall samurai as his father. At the same time his mind badgered him. It would indeed be a miraculous coincidence if the first high-ranking Heike that appeared at the swordsmith's door should not only turn out to be his father but should, in the course of an hour's discussion of swords, reveal this fact beyond doubt. Suddenly his dream seemed hopeless of fulfillment. How foolish he was to think that he could ever find his father! Takanobu had been right to ridicule him.

"See, Takanobu, I am no longer an empty-headed boy running after rainbows." *You haven't told me your name yet, puppy.* "Ah, Takanobu, that's it. If I stop searching for my father, I am nothing—No Name until the end of my days. But if I keep searching, there is at least the hope, and hope is better than nothing. Isn't it, Takanobu? Isn't it?"

Fukuji seemed preoccupied as he came through the kitchen on his way back to the forge.

"Did you sell a sword to the Heike samurai, sir?"

"What? Oh, no. It's not so simple as that, Muna." He hesitated in the doorway, then came back into the kitchen, seating himself on a wooden bench in the corner. "Have you wondered why I sell so few swords, boy?"

Muna flushed. "You make very wonderful blades, sir."

"No, that's not it." When Muna started to protest, the swordsmith put up his calloused hand. "Oh, the blades are true, but the men who would wear them. . . . Muna, the iron for the long sword comes from the belly of the earth. The metal is put to the test of the fire and the hammer and the water, and if it submits to the trials and endures, it emerges from the final tempering a pure and powerful spirit."

The swordsmith paused, searching the boy's face for a sign that Muna understood him. "So—" Fukuji continued, "I cannot bargain over a sword as though it were a . . . a piece of dried fish. I have to look at the man who would carry the sword, to try to see whether his spirit is worthy of the spirit of the blade."

"But a true samurai . . . ," the boy began.

"The capital is full of men who call themselves samurai these days. They squabble over women in the street—steal from their friends—set fire to the dwellings of their enemies. They are a dishonor to the swords they carry. I do not wish such a one to carry a sword with Fukuji engraved upon it." He rose abruptly. "Before you start the rice. . . ."

It took Muna a moment to realize that the lecture was over. The swordsmith smiled. "Before you start the rice, clear the tea things, will you?"

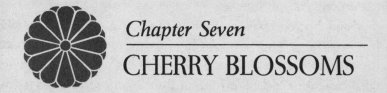

Chapter Seven

CHERRY BLOSSOMS

It was one of those exquisite April days that made every muscle of Muna's body lazy and happy. He wanted nothing more than to curl up under the plum tree and go to sleep with the buzz of insects in his ears and the smell of new leaves in his nostrils. As it was, he managed to sit there almost upright, his head nodding and jerking on his shoulders. The garment he had thought to mend lay in his lap. He could hear—it seemed miles away—the steady clang of Fukuji's hammer and even farther away the chatter of the street.

". . . and take in the blossom-viewing on the way." Suddenly there was Fukuji standing in front of him with something in his hand.

Muna jumped to his feet, murmuring excuses. The unmended garment fell to the cobblestones. "I'm sorry, sir. I'm afraid I didn't hear . . . ." He bent to pick it up.

"Yes, well. I have decided to forge a sword for Muratani of the Imperial Guards who was here recently. If you will take this note to him at the barracks, then you might return

55

through the Sanjo District and see the cherry blossoms and the crowds, if you like."

Muna bowed. He could hardly keep a smile of delight from his face. The barracks lay in the northeast section of the city, and even if he hurried, which Fukuji had said he need not, it would take him an hour or more to deliver the message. The swordsmith was giving him the afternoon to do as he pleased. He stuffed the note for Muratani in the fold of his tunic (he had a new one now, thanks to Fukuji), and stopping only to drop off the unmended garment in the house, he hurried into the narrow street toward the main avenue of Suzaku Oji.

The willow trees that lined the broad avenue bowed to the passersby like two lines of green-clad retainers. Muna had not been on the avenue since the night of his futile errand to Rashomon Gate. As he passed the intersection of Rokujo Avenue, the painful memory burned like fire in his chest.

Almost without realizing it, he made the turn toward the site of the Red Dog. Other shacklike buildings had been erected on the burned-out section of the street. It was as though the last trace of Takanobu had been blotted out. The boy turned and ran back toward Suzaku Oji.

Muna wondered as he neared the palace area whether anyone from the stables might see him. And then he had to smile. No one would recognize him. He wore the serviceable blue tunic and trousers of an artisan, and he knew that the hearty food of the swordsmith's kitchen had put flesh on his bones. His long black hair was bound back neatly at the back of his neck. He no longer aped the messy samurai topknot that had been the hallmark of Takanobu.

He inquired for the warrior Muratani, and when he appeared, Muna gave him the note from Fukuji. Muratani was delighted with the news and pressed some coins in the boy's hand for thanks. At first Muna politely declined the money, but the samurai insisted. "Go buy yourself some sweets at the cherry-viewing," he said. With a grin, Muna thanked him and was off.

The boughs of the cherry trees met in an arch above Sanjo Avenue. Muna walked beneath the pale pink arcade. It was as though all the ugliness he had ever known was excluded from this paradise. Even the people he saw seemed clothed in a glow of perfection. No one spoke loudly, but there was a quiet friendliness among the viewers. Here the proud and the poor mingled—court ladies in their flowing brocade robes, long black hair flowing to their waists, painted eyebrows and blackened teeth; street urchins, their faces and hands sticky with rice candy; samurai of the noble families in silk tunics with full trousers; artisans; peddlers; an occasional farmer with his mouth agape. They all belonged to one another under the sheltering branches of the cherry trees.

Muna bought a stick of rice candy from a peddler. The sweetness filled his mouth. It was the final goodness. He wanted to run and laugh and catch the falling blossoms on his face. He longed to see Takanobu and tell him of all the good fortune that had befallen a nameless country boy in this magnificent city. He wanted to tell his mother, old Sato, anyone, how happy he was.

Of course, Kawaki the sandalmaker. He would go to see him. And Akiko. What a good idea! With the rest of the samurai's coins, he bought rice sweets wrapped in a maple leaf.

The shutters of the sandal shop were open, but there was no one in sight. "Excuse me." Muna stepped up into the shop, leaving his sandals at street level. There was no answer to his call for a moment, and then Akiko appeared from behind the curtain that divided the shop from the living quarters.

She knelt and bowed politely on the mat, as though preoccupied, and apologized for keeping him waiting. She didn't recognize him, Muna realized. He was not sure whether he felt hurt or pleased.

"Akiko."

She lifted her face to look at him more closely. Muna smiled. "It's Muna. From Awa, remember?"

She cocked her head, and then lifted her small hand and smiled behind it. It was a beautiful gesture, Muna thought. She was growing up, too. Nearly a woman.

"It has been a long time," the boy apologized, "but today I was free and wanted to say thank you again for your kindness last summer." He pushed the sweets toward her.

She did not take them at once, but bowed her head formally to the floor, murmuring that his kindness was unnecessary.

"Is your father at home?" Muna asked.

The girl covered her mouth once more, but this time the gesture covered a little choked sound.

"Akiko?" A weak voice called from behind the curtain. "What is it, Akiko?"

The girl nodded toward Muna and led him through the curtain. There in the tiny back room old Kawaki lay propped up on his pallet bed. At the sight of the sandalmaker's face, the words of greeting froze on Muna's tongue. It was the wasting sickness. He knew. His mother had died of it. The bright spots in the cheeks.

"It is young Muna, Father," the girl said.

"I see. I see," said the man. His weak voice was warm with welcome.

He raised his thin hand from the quilt and indicated Muna's clothes. "So you found the fortune you came to seek in the capital, eh, boy?"

Muna shook his head. "I have a good master."

"A good master is better than good luck," Kawaki replied. "What trade are you learning?"

The boy flushed. He was tempted to lie, but found he could not. "I am in the house of Fukuji the swordsmith, but he has not made me his apprentice—yet."

"Fukuji?" Kawaki licked his parched lips, his eyes were

shining. "He is the greatest swordsmith in the capital. You have come into a fortune, Muna."

Akiko had brought in tea to go with the rice sweets. Her eyes shone, too.

"Did you hear who Muna's master is, Akiko?" The old man half raised himself up from the pallet.

The girl nodded, handing Muna his tea with a little bow. He thought for a moment that her fingertips would touch his, and his hand began to shake. But she did not touch him after all.

He spoke to cover his confusion. "I cannot tell if he will make me an apprentice. He is very exacting."

"Of course," replied Kawaki. "His genius demands perfection, but don't be discouraged, a fine boy like you . . . ." He dropped back against Akiko's arm. The girl supported Kawaki with one arm and with the other hand held his tea-cup as he took a few sips. How gentle she was. Muna remembered with pain his own clumsy attempts to nurse his mother. What would Kawaki do without her? What rather, the thought rushed into his mind like a wave to the shore, what would she do without Kawaki?

When he excused himself a few minutes later, Akiko followed him to the street. Muna longed to ask her what she
would do when her father died, but how could he?

"He is dying," the girl said simply as soon as they were out
of Kawaki's hearing.

Muna mumbled a protest.

"No, I am sure," she said.

"If he should die," Muna stumbled over the words, "what
will happen to you?"

The girl kept her eyes on her sandals. "I have an
uncle . . . ," she said vaguely, her voice trailing off. "I must
not leave him," she said, bowing quickly.

Muna bowed his head in return, but he kept his eyes on
Akiko. "I'll come again," he promised. "The first free day."

"It would cheer him." Her voice broke as she spoke. She
turned and disappeared into the house.

From the height of the sun, Muna could tell that it was
nearly time for supper. He hurried his pace a bit, for it was a
good distance to Fukuji's from this part of town. His mood,
as he turned into the jostling traffic of Suzaku Oji, was quite
different from what he had felt a few hours before. He was
burdened now with a concern for Kawaki, who had been so
kind to him that first miserable night in the capital, and for
Akiko, who would soon be an orphan like himself. It was like
the song that Fukuji sang.

> *Has this world*
> *Been from ancient days*
> *Full of sorrow?*
> *Or has it become so*
> *For me alone?*

Yet as he turned the words over in his mind, he was conscious of a feeling—a feeling as real as the taste of rice-stick candy in his mouth a few hours before. It was a consciousness of the great sorrow in the world of which his own misfortunes were only a tiny part. The world had been from ancient days full of sorrow. But not until today had he been able to look up from his own troubled portion of it long enough to see that he was not alone. It was a new feeling, and although Muna could not say why, it was not an unhappy one.

"Watch where you're going, fool!" Muna looked up, startled, into the face of the man he had walked into. There was a moment of confusion as both man and boy stared. The man began to move away quickly.

"Koishi!" Muna called after him. But the man had disappeared. Muna began to run, calling as he went. "Koishi! It's me, Muna. Wait!"

The boy paid no attention to the cursing of the persons he pushed aside. He was sure the man he had bumped into was Koishi, whom he had thought dead in the ashes of the Red Dog. But perhaps he was mistaken, for no one turned when he called. He saw a back which he was sure belonged to Takanobu's friend, but when he caught up with the man, the face was strange.

That evening Fukuji seemed kinder than usual. He did not ask Muna where he had been, but instead recalled times in the past when he himself had gone to view the blossoms in the Sanjo District of the city.

As the swordsmith talked, Muna ate the food Fukuji had prepared, debating with himself whether to confide the events of the day to his master. Should he tell him of Kawaki and Akiko? But if he did, would Fukuji think that he was asking help for them, people for whom Fukuji had no obligation, and should he mention the man on Suzaku Oji who so resembled Koishi? Muna had told the swordsmith very little of his previous life in the city—simply that a ronin he had met on shipboard had found him employment at the stables, but that the man had died in the New Year's Eve fire. Nor had he dared tell Fukuji about his father and the dream he had of finding him in the capital. He had thought it better to wait until he was sure the swordsmith trusted him.

But tonight the spring air seemed to invade even the steel spirit of Fukuji. Tonight the boy might dare approach him. Muna bowed over his soup bowl, using his chopsticks to guide the bits of fish and vegetable into his mouth. Over the rim of the bowl he watched the swordsmith, wondering how to begin.

He cleared his throat. Fukuji raised his eyes expectantly.

"Excuse me!" A call from the front of the shop broke the moment. Muratani had come to discuss the new sword.

By the time he left, Muna was sure that he ought to wait. There was no reason now that he should approach the older man with his own affairs. Later, perhaps, when he had proved his worth to the swordsmith. When he was more than a yardsweep—when the swordsmith recognized that he was becoming a man, then he would speak.

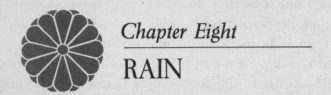

Chapter Eight

RAIN

The rains came in early summer, and the season seemed more dreary than any year Muna could remember. Fukuji kept the forge fire burning much of the time, and the smoke, unable to rise in the humid atmosphere, glutted the house and courtyard. The smell permeated clothes, bedding, food —everything.

There was a heaviness within the boy as well. He knew that Kawaki was sure to die. The old man coughed blood and was scarcely able to eat.

Muna had been to the sandal shop twice since the cherry blossoms fell, and each time he sank deeper into despair. The uncle of whom Akiko had spoken was there the second time. The man had brought food and herb medicines, but Akiko seemed more apprehensive than grateful. "He never gives anything without expecting repayment," the girl explained. But with what could Kawaki and Akiko repay him? The uncle already owned the sandal shop. Kawaki had deeded that over to him during the long illness of Akiko's mother. There was very little stock, for Kawaki, of course, was unable to work; and Akiko spent most of her time trying to keep him comfortable.

The two of them were constantly in Muna's mind. As he fanned the fire in the charcoal brazier, he could see Akiko at the same task. She had a way of pushing her long, thick hair away from her eyes with her left hand as she knelt before the brazier, the blur of the fan keeping perfect rhythm in her right hand. What lovely hands they were—slender fingers that moved with such grace that Muna couldn't help but stare. Chopping a cucumber—the knife flick-flick-flick under her tiny hand, turning the green vegetable miraculously into scores of incandescent slices.

Muna tried now in Fukuji's kitchen to imitate the deft movement; but his hands were clumsy, and the slices came out in uneven hunks. He nearly cut himself trying to slice the fat pieces into thin ones. "Stupid fool," he said aloud, dropping the knife on the wooden board in disgust.

It was raining again. The smoke hung so heavily in the courtyard that Muna could hardly make out the outline of the forge. *Clang! Clang! Clang!* Fukuji had shut himself into the forge to work on the sword for Muratani. It never seemed to occur to the man how hateful that closed door was to Muna. The boy listened to the ring of the hammer, which seemed to hit him with a kind of pain. Would Fukuji never open the forge door to him?

The swordsmith was kind to him as always, and lately he had begun to give the boy a wage of sorts. But he never gave any indication that he would offer Muna an apprenticeship —or even that he might be considering it.

"You'd better spread out all the bedding. Everything is likely to mildew in this weather," Fukuji said over his rice bowl at noon.

"Yes, sir." Muna hesitated. "And then may I go out for a while?"

"As you like." The swordsmith poured tea into the last grains of rice in his bowl and lifted it to his mouth and drank it down. "Warms the belly on a day like this, eh?"

Muna was surprised and pleased. It was seldom that Fukuji betrayed his country origins. Tea on rice was a peasant's treat. It lifted the boy's spirits. When he followed the swordsmith's example, Fukuji smiled and fetched them both a dried plum pickle.

"It is a feast, sir." The sourness of the plum made the boy's eyes squint up. He slurped in the tea and rice with noisy peasant pleasure.

"Why did you leave your nest before your wings were dry?"

Muna looked up, startled.

"You are not obliged to answer my question," the swordsmith continued. "It was presumptuous of me."

"I—I came to seek my father. My mother is dead, so I have no one else."

"And she told you he was here in the capital?"

The boy nodded, not daring to look at Fukuji. "He is a Heike warrior."

"Does he know you?"

"No."

"Forgive me, Muna, but there are many Heike warriors in the capital. If you meet your father, how will you know him?"

The boy kept his eyes averted. "He has a small tattoo—my mother told me—a chrysanthemum—on his left shoulder."

"I see. Then perhaps you should seek employment in the public bath rather than a swordsmith's shop."

It was meant as a joke; at least, Muna hoped so.

"Yes, well," he said in unconscious mimic of Fukuji. They both laughed then.

When he had rinsed the bowls and chopsticks and spread bedding all over the floors of both front rooms, Muna put on a straw rain cape and started out for the sandal shop.

Fukuji's kindness at noon had lifted his spirits immeasurably. In addition he had two coins, his weekly wage, to share with Kawaki and Akiko. On impulse he took a detour toward Rashomon Gate. Instead of food, this time he would buy something simply to make Akiko happy. Like Fukuji's pickled plum. He poked about the stalls in Thieves' Market until he found just the thing—a tiny goldfish swimming in a bowl fashioned from a section of bamboo.

"I've brought you a friend, so you won't be lonely." Muna took the present from behind his back and handed it to Akiko.

"For me? You should not do this." She pushed her hair back from her face.

"No, no. You must take it," he urged her.

She hesitated a moment and then reached out with both hands. "My"—she studied the little creature, flicking its graceful tail as it went round and round the bamboo section —"My"—she smiled at Muna—"I shall keep it forever."

The boy blushed with pleasure. "It is nothing," he mumbled.

The uncle was with Kawaki, so Muna spoke only a few awkward words to the sick man. He noticed that Akiko did not bring the fish in to show to the two men. The uncle asked after Muna's master in an unctuous manner that made the boy uneasy. It was plain to see that Kawaki was worse. But Muna had given Akiko a few moments of delight. No one could take that away from either of them, Muna comforted himself as he set out for home.

As he left the house, he noticed a monk lounging about the gate of the temple next door. It was as though the man were waiting for someone, though his posture seemed at odds with his robe. As Muna went past, the man straightened. Was he following? As absurd as it seemed, whenever Muna quickened his pace, a glance over his shoulder showed the monk hurrying. When he slowed, the monk slowed.

Muna began to run. The monk began to run. Then suddenly Muna stopped and whirled. The monk ran straight into him, nearly knocking him over.

"Ah, but that was sly, puppy!"

"Takanobu!" Forgetting his age and the little dignity he had acquired, Muna threw his arms about the ronin as though he were a child.

"Where have you been?" the ronin demanded, giving him a playful swat. "I thought you were dead—until Koishi thought he saw you one day on Suzaku Oji."

"I thought *you* were dead." The boy grinned happily. "And I wasn't sure I'd even seen Koishi. When I called to him, he ran."

"What a rogue! Come, let's find a wineshop, and you can tell me why you deserted me last year." Takanobu was as ebullient as ever.

"You haven't taken the tonsure?" Muna asked, indicating the robe. The shop was dark, and the wine cheap.

"What? Oh, the robe? A man must wear something in the rain, hey?" He emptied his cup.

"But—" Muna hesitated. "Your sword. Where's your sword?"

For a moment a flicker of concern crossed the ronin's features. Then he threw out his palm in a gesture of dice play and shrugged his shoulders. "Now tell me about yourself," he said.

Muna rubbed the bottom of his cup across his knee. "I am as you see," he said. Takanobu had lost his sword in a dice game! And he called himself a samurai. Had the man no honor?

"I see that fortune has been kinder to you than to me." The ronin wiped his mouth and moustache with the back of his hand.

"I didn't mean to desert you, Takanobu. When I came back to the tavern that night, there was nothing there. I thought you had all died. I nearly died myself."

"Oh?"

"If it had not been for Fukuji the swordsmith. . . ."

"And where are you living now, puppy?" The ronin signaled for more wine.

"I am there still." The girl filled his cup. Takanobu waited until she had left and then leaned toward the boy.

"With all your good fortune, would you be willing to help your old friend?"

"Of course."

"As you see, I need a sword . . . ."

"But . . . ."

"I don't have the money right now, but naturally . . . ."

A chill went through the boy. He knew that Fukuji would never sell a sword to Takanobu even if by some miracle he did have the money.

"I'm not even an apprentice. I don't even touch the

swords. I'm sorry, Takanobu. I wish I could help you, but I don't have any influence with my master. He's a very strange and harsh man." Muna began to lie desperately against the fear of the next request the ronin might make.

"I might well have died in that fire. No thanks to you who would have left me dying in the ashes."

Muna stared incredulously at the ronin. There had been no one left when he saw the ashes of the Red Dog. . . . Or had there been? That terrible smoke.

"But my life might as well be over—without a sword I am nothing. You know that." Takanobu gulped down the dregs of the wine. "As you can see I have no money now with which to buy a sword—not even a poor weapon like the one I once carried. And even if I did have money—" He set his cup down carefully. "How could I persuade Fukuji to make a blade for me? What would such a man see when he looked at me? What do you see? A swordless ronin, a nothing, hardly more than a ragpicker at Rashomon Gate." He paused, but Muna could not deny his argument. "But"—he leaned forward—"with a sword of Fukuji at my belt, what do I become?" The ronin threw back his head. "A prince among warriors! A divinity! No man or god would dare despise such a weapon nor the samurai who wore it." He leaned forward once more, his face flushed dark red in the dim light. "My life is once again in your hands."

"But there is nothing I can do," Muna protested. "If you had had any respect for a sword, you would not have lost yours gambling."

"Your own father"—the ronin shook his head sadly—"your own father. Is this your revenge, my son?"

"You're lying again!" Muna jumped to his feet, his body shaking with rage. "Don't torture me with your cruel jokes. I'm no longer a boy."

The ronin remained cross-legged on the floor. "I should have told you before, but when I saw you had such a grandiose dream of your father, I didn't have the heart."

"But now you need something from me," said the boy angrily.

"Exactly." The ronin's voice was humble. "Otherwise, I would not have bothered you again."

"You've known all along where I was?" Muna was close to tears of exasperation.

"For a few months."

"I have to go. My master expects me."

"Will you at least think about my request—son?" Muna winced at the ronin's word. "I will repay the money as soon as I am able."

Muna looked away from the earnest face and nodded. He started for the door.

"By my honor!" The ronin stood there both hands in the air, a crooked smile on his face. Muna turned and ran into the driving rain.

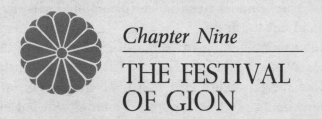

Chapter Nine

THE FESTIVAL OF GION

He had promised to think about Takanobu's request. By the gods, if only for one moment he could think about anything else! He was like an animal caught between two opposing lines of bowmen—all of the arrows flying toward him.

Of what could he be sure now? That he had once had a father. That, at least. That his father had been a warrior? Probably. His guileless mother could hardly have invented the whole tale. That his father was a high-ranking Heike samurai? At this point his body grew hot, and he wanted to twist away from the painful questioning, but he forced himself to face it. Was his father a high-ranking samurai? No, more likely his father had been the imaginative one, inventing that detail to impress the one at his side, so eager to be impressed. Perhaps—just perhaps—he was a ronin who sold his sword to ship captains in fear of pirates, a rogue who amused himself in port with country girls that listened wide-eyed to his charming lies. *The chrysanthemum, why hadn't he asked to see it?*

A vision flashed across Muna's mind—a vision of his mother, his little childlike mother, with Takanobu. Muna passed his hand before his face as if to bat the scene away. But if not Takanobu, *someone like Takanobu*. That was a bur he could not brush off.

Takanobu himself hung to Muna like a bur during the next weeks. Muna would scarcely have left the swordsmith's shop before the tall figure clad as a monk would fall into step beside him. "I can't wait, puppy. You must not put me off." The ronin spread a large hand on his chest. "Your own father."

But Muna *did* put him off. To steal a sword from Fukuji was too unthinkable.

Meanwhile the rice seedlings of the rainy season were stretching green heads up above the paddies toward the sun. Beyond the fields, through the veil of midsummer haze, the mountains surrounding the capital were lush with green as well.

The festival of Gion was at hand. At Fukuji's suggestion, Muna went to the great Gion Shrine to see the parade and the fortunate boy who had been chosen to be this year's sacred page.

The festival of Gion was devoted to Susano, the storm-god, that "swift-impetuous deity" who could never be counted on. Sometimes he was a great hero, slaying the dragons that plagued mankind, but as often as not he was a naughty boy playing pranks on his noble sister Amaterasu, goddess of the sun. The impetuous warriors and fickle courtiers of Heiankyo found him an appropriate object for their devotion.

Muna jostled his way to the front of the crowd for a better view of the gorgeous procession as it neared the shrine's torii (the gateway of two tall posts and two horizontal ones through which a shrine is approached). Riding on a white war-horse was a boy of about his own age—but there the resemblance ended. This boy was perfect of feature, his complexion fair, as one who has always been protected from the elements. He wore a red silk brocaded outer garment, the loops of the full sleeves betraying a gold inner lining. His full puffed trousers were of delicate blue silk, like the blue of an April sky. His long hair was bound up under a tall black court cap. And at his side hung a long sword in a jeweled sheath.

The *chigo*—the sacred page of the festival—held his boyish face in a mask of modesty, but as he passed under the torii, Muna could see the pride in his straight back. And why should he not be proud? Of all the sons of the great families of the city, he alone had been chosen to dance the sacred dance of the Gion Shrine and for the nine days of the festival to bear in his person the spirit of the gods.

"He is the *chigo*, the sacred page of the gods, while I—I am the nameless one, the nothing of man or god." Muna's eyes dropped to his square peasant feet.

An elbow jabbed his ribs. "Impressive, eh?" Takanobu was standing beside him. Muna felt a scrape of annoyance. Now his holiday was stolen.

"I *must* have the sword by the end of the festival." The ronin spoke through his clenched teeth, so that in the din of the crowd he would not be overheard.

"I cannot." The flutes of the passing musicians wailed mournfully.

"You must understand." Takanobu kept his eyes on the

procession as he continued. "It is not for me alone. The city is set for revolt. It may come anytime." A drunken samurai stumbled past with a woman on his arm. "Anytime, that is, after some of us sober up from the holidays."

"Revolt?" *Donk-donk, dada, donk-donk* warned the passing drums.

"Hush, fool." The ronin glanced about, then leaned closer

to the boy. "On the Street of the Ox Dealers, the shop just north of the Fox Shrine. I will be waiting on the last night of the festival." He looked into Muna's troubled face with his eyes flashing. "For the Emperor, if not for me!" And he shoved off into the throng of merrymakers.

Donk-donk, dada, donk-donk. The procession moved on under the torii into the shrine grounds. Muna watched the gaily dressed musicians, the samurai on horseback, but in his mind he was rehearsing a scene with Fukuji.

"It is an impossible entreaty I make, but . . . ." No. "For the sake of the Emperor and the city, could you . . . ?" Again no. He had no illusions that Takanobu acted out of love for the Emperor.

But why, why, he wondered, was he so concerned for Fukuji? The swordsmith had promised him nothing. Surely Muna had repaid his debt of honor by now in doing thousands of menial tasks during these past six months. Must he have nothing more to look forward to in life than woman's work? Whereas, if he went to Takanobu with a sword. . . . *Donk-donk, dada, donk-donk.* His heart skipped with the drum beat. Other men had made their names in battle. . . . Yet if there were any hope that Fukuji would make him an apprentice. . . . But suppose Takanobu were in truth his father . . . ?

His mind reeled under the clash of opposing arguments. The crowd was pressing into the shrine grounds now, but the boy began to push through in the opposite direction. He would soon be fifteen and accounted a man. Somewhere in this narrow land there must be a place for him—or must he make his own place? That was it. The luckless must snatch their own luck. He elbowed and ducked a passage through the surging crowd. That was it. He was nearly a man, and a man must make his own place to stand—must seize his own fortune.

The swordsmith was seated at the grindstone. So he had completed the final tempering of Muratani's sword. "Is that why he wanted me out of the way? Did he fear I'd snatch his precious secrets through a closed door?" thought Muna.

"How was it?" The grizzled head stayed bent over the wheel as Fukuji spoke. He kept the blade delicately balanced as he pumped rhythmically to keep the grindstone in motion.

"As always," replied the boy coolly, so intent on his pique that he forgot that he had never seen the festival before.

The swordsmith did not remind him.

Muna toed a cobblestone with the tip of his sandal. "Are you nearly through with Muratani's sword?"

"Just the grinding and polishing. By the end of the festival . . . ."

Muna sucked in his breath. Was it a sign from the gods? He kicked an imaginary stone.

"What is it, Muna?"

"I—that is, at the New Year I shall be fifteen."

"So?" Fukuji continued the grinding. The blade caught sunlight and flashed in Muna's eyes.

"I shall be a man."

"Yes, well . . . ."

Curse his coolness. "I must know what you are thinking of me, Fukuji."

The swordsmith lifted the blade and seemed to study its surface. "What *I* think of you?"

"Yes." The boy stumbled on. "Will you make me your apprentice?"

The silence rose and grew like the approach of a tidal wave. Muna wanted to turn and flee before it overwhelmed him, but he willed his feet to stand against the fearful flood.

At last the silence broke, crashing in upon his stiff body. "My child," said Fukuji. "The proper question must be, What do you think of yourself?"

My child. *Child. Child.* Muna thought that he would be overwhelmed, suffocated, but the man continued his quiet assault.

"If you are not content with yourself, what does it matter what I think?" The sharp eyes went back to the blade. The sure, strong foot began the rhythmic pedaling once more.

Was this to be his answer? By the gods, he deserved better than this. The protests stammered inside his head. *Look at me! Fukuji, save me!*

But the conversation was over.

Without a word, without a "by your leave," the boy left. Akiko. She would help him. She did not think him a stupid child. She would listen to him. He began to run, his hair streaming behind him like a war banner.

Donk-donk, dada, donk-donk. Donk-donk, dada, donk-donk. They had nothing but contempt for him. Takanobu. Fukuji. They used him. Puppy. Child. He was nothing to them. *Donk-donk, dada, donk-donk.* Akiko would not despise him. He had to see her. He had to know he was someone. Angry tears started in his eyes.

From the sandal-shop doorway came noises of laughter and the raucous tone of conversation that signals celebration. With Kawaki so near death? How dare they?

"Akiko!" He almost bellowed her name at the door.

"Ah, the swordsmith's boy." The uncle greeted him with an elaborate bow, a cup of rice wine in his pudgy hand.

"Akiko?" It was almost a whisper this time.

"Ah, yes. Well, I'm afraid, my boy, that our sorrowful news has yet to reach your ears." The effusive politeness was maddening. "Our beloved Kawaki, husband to my late sister, some eight days before the opening of the festival . . . ."

"Akiko. Where is Akiko?" A great fear had seized the boy, and his whole body began to shake.

"We have been most fortunate." The uncle coughed importantly. "She is quite well situated."

"Where?" cried Muna, strangling on the word.

"Yes. A lovely house it is. One of the largest on Rokujo Avenue, just a step off Suzaku Oji." He swished the warm wine around in his cup, completely oblivious to the agonies through which Muna was passing. "She has always been a pretty little thing, you know. Really wasted in a sandal shop."

"I must leave," thought Muna, "before I kill him." Somewhere in the distance a single flute wailed its sorrow to the unfeeling sky.

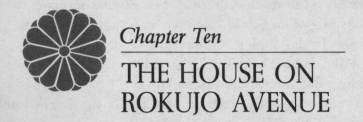

Chapter Ten

THE HOUSE ON ROKUJO AVENUE

There was a bitter taste of bile in his mouth as he ran down Suzaku Oji, his head thumping with every step as though a large rock were being bounced from one side of his skull to the other.

Akiko, Akiko. He had no plan—no more cunning than a raging bear whose cub has been stolen. He simply ran to where he thought she might be, determined to snatch her away to safety.

When he got to the intersection, he turned right. A large house, the uncle had said, just a step off Suzaku Oji. The street was already crowded with merrymakers from the festival, seeking to crown their day with a night in the bawdy district.

Muna elbowed his way through to the doorway of the largest house. On the threshold stood a woman in a garish kimono, her face powdered to a ghostly white upon which eyebrows and lips were painted. Her mouth curved into an exaggerated smile. She stuck out a long arm and barred the entrance. "First you pay, little one. Then you are welcome to come in."

Muna's throat was so dry that he could hardly speak, and his body still heaved from the exertion of running such a distance.

"Akiko," he gasped out. "Daughter of Kawaki the sandalmaker. Is she here?"

The woman laughed a shrill mirthless laugh. "First you pay."

"I have no money!" he cried. "Please, please, help me. I have to find her."

"No money?" The painted eyebrows went up. "Kato!" she called sharply into the house.

A burly man appeared, the hulk of his body filling the narrow doorway. The woman jerked her head toward Muna and dropped her arm. The man took a step toward him, legs spread like a wrestler, his huge muscled arms held out from his body, poised. But Muna was too quick. He ducked around the mountainous form into the dim interior.

"Akiko!" he screamed the name. "Akiko!"

Heads popped out of every entranceway, powdered faces staring. Suddenly a girl appeared. She was wearing a bright red-and-lavender kimono, her hair piled high off her neck. Her face, like all the others, was an eerie white with black blots for eyebrows and a red wound for a mouth. When she opened her mouth to speak, she revealed blackened teeth.

"Go away, Muna." It was she. *Merciful Kwannon, what had they done?* "Quickly! Please, I beg you, go away."

"Akiko!" He reached out to grab her arm. He must get her away from this terrible place. But as his hand touched her sleeve, there was a sharp pain on the back of his head. He was dimly aware that the one called Kato was dragging him out behind the house.

There, armed with only his massive right hand, Kato
began to beat him, coldly and systematically. The pain en-
gulfed him like a dark cave, but in the tiny corner of his consciousness that remained to him, Muna acknowledged a kind

of admiration for the man's workmanship. He went about his task like a craftsman, plying his trade with small grunts of concentration and the natural cadence of a true artist. Muna clenched his teeth and forced his mind from the pain to the rhythmic sound of flesh on flesh.

Suddenly it was over. Kato was wiping his great hands on his apron. "Now," he said and the words buzzed in Muna's head. "Now, you filthy little son of nothing. You try a trick like this again, and I'll beat the girl—just as I've beaten you tonight. As for you"—he spat. The cold spittle stung Muna's burning skin—"Who knows what I might do to you!"

He grabbed the boy by an arm and leg and threw him into the alley. Somewhere, miles away, Muna heard a door slam and voices laughing, but the buzzing in his head grew louder and blocked out every other sound.

"I am going to die." The thought cut through the buzzing and burning, crystal and cool.

"No." He heard his voice raspy and weak. He forced it to be strong. "No." He struggled to his feet, only to fall again. For a long time he lay there, the slightest movement sending a thrill of pain through his body. Then like a war-horse, with a great shudder he forced himself once more to his feet, and grasping the sides of buildings for support, made his way back to the swordsmith's shop.

At dawn he dragged himself from between his quilts and went about his duties. All day he could feel the swordsmith watching him, asking with his eyes the meaning of his bruises. But the boy said nothing. He would give no hint to his master of the raging spirit locked in the cage of aching, burning flesh.

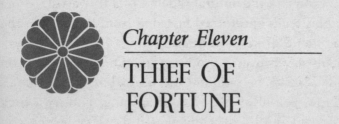

Chapter Eleven
THIEF OF FORTUNE

Gentle Akiko. They have destroyed you. Behind the lattice windows of Rokujo Avenue. Just a few coins! If I could kill them all, I would. If I could free you, I swear to the gods, I would. You know I cannot. But they will not get me—that, at least, I promise. I will use them as they have used me. I will snatch my fortune from their grasping hands. They will not crush us both.

During the next few days, Muna went about his daily tasks at the swordsmith's with an efficiency that would have surprised him had he thought about it. Fukuji's orders, even his desires, were anticipated. Nothing was forgotten or left half done, but every job was completed beyond expectation. The boy worked with feverish intensity—his features immobile, his lips silent.

At last the inner storm subsided. His heart was silent, too. It was as though, having made his decision, he must shove out any memory that might cause him reflection or pain and slam a heavy gate against any whisper of remorse.

Muna did not watch the swordsmith at work in the courtyard, not with his eyes. But the boy was acutely aware of every stage of the grinding and polishing. The hilt, with its delicately filigreed guard, and the sheath, upon which a spray of chrysanthemums had been painted in gold leaf, had been delivered from the craftsmen entrusted with their creation. It would not be long now.

Two days before the end of the festival, the swordsmith stood facing the east and raised the blade toward the morning sun, as if to say "See, O Amaterasu, what your son has brought forth from the fire and water." Then he called the boy to examine the finished sword.

Muna gasped. He could not help himself. The slightly curved blade had been ground and polished so that three distinct hues gave back the radiance of the sun. Noon shone in the highly gleaming polish near the ridge and back of the sword; at the cutting edge, a grayish twilight; and between the two, an area like sunlight trying to pierce the snow clouds of a winter afternoon.

"Ahhh." Muna reached out for a moment under the spell of the flawless blade; but he caught himself and pulled back his hand. "Shall I take word to Muratani that the sword is ready?"

"Um." The swordsmith nodded. "I have just the final engraving left. I have yet to settle on a suitable motto for this beauty. Tell him that tomorrow, by evening, I should have finished."

A quiet exultancy rose within the boy. His plan was going even better than he had hoped.

Muna walked quickly to the barracks, going out of his way to avoid walking past the intersection of Suzaku Oji and Rojujo Avenue—*Had she taken the goldfish with her?*—Sternly Muna rid his mind of thoughts that might weaken him. When he had power and a name to be reckoned with, he would return.

The samurai Muratani did not try to hide his disappointment at the message Muna brought. "But I'd hoped," the guardsman said, "that the sword would be ready by the end of the festival . . . ."

"My master regrets the delay."

Although lying was a new skill for Muna, he was perversely pleased to see how easily his tongue took to it. "On the other hand, neither you nor he would be satisfied with less than a perfect blade. By the end of summer, he is sure to have another made. Although"—he consciously inserted a knowledgeable dimension to his voice—"one can never tell how a blade will emerge from the final tempering, you know."

"Of course," Muratani agreed. "Convey my regards." He slapped some coins in the boy's hand as was his custom. This time Muna did not hesitate to accept them. "Until next month then?"

"Until next month." The boy bowed and took his leave.

"But I thought he was so eager for the sword . . . ." Fukuji tugged his beard in puzzlement at the boy's message that Muratani would not come to fetch the sword for another month or more.

"Oh, yes. His friend said he would come as soon as he returns."

"Did he say what the trouble on Mount Hiei was all about?"

Muna had prepared for this question and answered it

smoothly. "The warrior-priests. It is rumored that they are preparing another foray against the capital. So Lord Kiyomori has sent Muratani and some of his retainers to investigate."

"Those plagued priests. As if Genji and Heike did not bring us grief enough." Fukuji rose from the low table where he had been sitting, the sword before him, and placed the blade carefully into its sheath. "But at least I have more time to think about the motto."

Muna watched from the kitchen doorway as the swordsmith retrieved the storehouse key from under a loose stone. Then Fukuji opened the heavy door and placed the sword on a shelf inside the storehouse.

"It will be days before Fukuji discovers it is gone. By the time he misses it, it will be far away indeed. For," thought the boy with grim satisfaction, "it will not occur to him that I might steal it."

Clack, clack, clack-clack. A lone watchman passed in the street, clapping his wooden blocks and calling out in his mournful voice of night: "It is the hour of the sheep. Watch for fires. Watch for fires." *Clack, clack, clack-clack.* He repeated his call as he went on through the empty streets. In the distance a dog barked.

Muna raised himself up on his elbows and listened to the steady breathing of the man on the pallet under the wall of swords. At last the boy slid out from under the light summer quilt. He was fully dressed, except for his sandals. Keeping his eyes on the sleeping form, he crept out toward the kitchen. On the step he stumbled. *Dunk.* It was barely a sound, but the swordsmith turned in his sleep.

For a long time Muna stood still as death on the stair. He

tried not to breathe, but the beating of his heart sounded like a festival drum inside his ears. When, finally, it seemed that Fukuji was not going to move again, the boy stepped down and slid the door open inch by inch until he could slip out through the narrow opening into the moonlit courtyard.

Muna dug under the loose stone for the key. Silently he slid back the heavy bolt of the door and entered the storehouse. It was black as a grave and musty-smelling, for there were no windows. By feel and memory Muna located the shelf and patted its length until his fingers finally curled about the sword. The pulse in his temple thudded painfully now, as he left the storehouse, relocked the door, put the key back under the stone, and stole out the courtyard gate into the street beyond.

He had no sooner pushed the gate shut behind than a sharp sensation of cold went through his feet. It took him a

moment, standing in the dark, to locate the pain, for at the time all his body functions seemed labored and painful. Then he knew what he had done. His sandals. He had left them at the kitchen door.

He cursed his stupidity, but he dared not go back for them. Where he could get more, he did not know, but for now he must make his way over the rough stone streets barefooted. It couldn't be helped.

In the shadow of the gate Muna loosened the sash bound around his tunic and trousers, and slipped the sword down inside his trouser leg. Then he bound the sash again over both tunic and trousers. The sword bumped against his leg at every step, but at length he became accustomed to the pain in his feet and the thudding of the sword, and found them oddly satisfying, like a pilgrim taking pride in his penance as he makes the itinerary of the shrines. "But," he said to himself wryly, "my journey is not a holy one."

Even had there been no moon, he would have found the Street of the Ox Dealers without difficulty. One simply (as the saying went) crossed Suzaku Oji and followed his nose. Each area of the city had its peculiar odors, but here the odor of the oxen and their droppings laced the stench of human poverty. Muna was not squeamish, but the nature of his mission, combined with the assault on his nostrils and the filth clinging to his feet, dragged his spirit to the edge of despair.

But he did not turn back. How could he? He passed the Fox Shrine. One of the guardians was etched, sharp nose and pointed ears, against the moonlight. His heart stopped. This was the place.

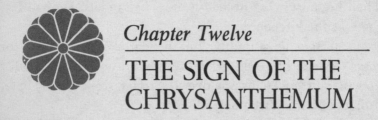

Chapter Twelve

THE SIGN OF THE CHRYSANTHEMUM

The shop was completely shuttered. No light shone through the cracks. Muna hesitated for a moment. What if—an icicle pierced his belly—what if Takanobu spurned his demand? Muna shook off the question. It was impossible that the ronin should refuse. For a Fukuji sword, Takanobu would do anything.

He put his mouth close to the shutter and called in a low voice. "Takanobu?"

He waited, not knowing whether to pray that the ronin was there or not. Perhaps he could still run. Then he heard the shuffling of feet. The shutter slid back, and a woman's face appeared.

"Takanobu—the warrior Takanobu is expecting me."

The woman simply nodded and moved to let him pass into the entryway.

"Follow me."

Awkwardly Muna scraped his feet on the hard-packed dirt of the entryway, then climbed up into the shop, following the woman across the tiny front room and through the cur-

tains. In the back room, lit only by a single oil lamp, sat a circle of men. Every face turned toward him as he entered.

"Ha! Didn't I tell you he'd come?" Takanobu leaped up
from the shadowy circle and came toward him. "Welcome,
puppy, welcome!" He slapped Muna on the back. Then he
leaned toward him, his breath foul with cheap wine. "The
sword. Where is the sword?" he hoarsely whispered.

Muna struck his side where the sword was concealed. Even
in the dim light he knew that every eye was on him, and he
did not like the feel of it. "I need to talk to you—in private,"
he said in a low voice.

The ronin threw a glance at his companions, then with a
nod, led the boy back into the street.

"Let me have it," he said.

Muna loosened his sash and drew out the sword; Takanobu extended his big hand, his body taut with eagerness,
but the boy held the sword aside.

"I brought you this sword because you said you were my
father," Muna said.

Instinctively the ronin stepped back.

"Whether or not you are truly my father, I will know soon
enough. But if you are willing to be my father for the sake of
this sword—then—then swear upon its blade that you will
from this night regard me as your son. Swear—swear that I
may follow you into battle or wherever fortune may lead
you. Swear"—the boy's voice rose—"swear that you will give
me the name of your family."

The tall man stood speechless, his form black against the
night sky. Muna could not see his face. Now that he had
thrown out the demand, he could only wait. The speech had

exhausted his bravado. Cold sweat poured over his body. His feet throbbed with pain.

"*Har, har, har!*" The body of the ronin shook under his powerful laughter. "You fool!" he said. "You little country fool! Do you think for one moment I would tie you about my neck like a great temple bell?" He began to sway his body in imitation. "Dragging me down and clanging to my destruction?" He leaned forward once more, and this time Muna could see the burning eyes above the brierlike beard.

"Now let me have the sword and be off—like a good puppy."

But the boy stood his ground, clinging to the sword. "So you are not my father."

"I might be—anyone might. Why not me, puppy?"

Fury whipped within the boy's body. He snatched the sword from the sheath and raised it. No laughter now.

"No. No." the ronin held out his hand. "Now hand it over. Gently—there's a good puppy. . . ."

Muna swung down heavily. Takanobu leaped backward, but the drink had dulled him. Muna watched in horror a black rivulet spring up from the back of the ronin's hand.

He began to run. Clutching the sword in one hand and the sheath in the other, he ran without thought for his bruised feet. Terror drove him.

From the Imperial Palace at the north to Rashomon Gate at the south runs the Suzaki Oji—the broad avenue from Heaven to Hell. Muna turned south; stopping only to rebind the sword under his garment, he headed for Rashomon. The great gate thrust its giant hulk into the night, while at its feet in gray clusters lay the offal of the city, trying to forget misery in sleep. Terror crumbled into weariness.

Muna picked his way around and across the huddled forms until he found a space almost large enough for himself. He could not curl up, for the sword bound him from his waist to his feet like some strange instrument of torture, requiring him to lie perfectly straight. But the place was too short; so with the sword under him, the guard cutting into his flesh, he lay, arms across his chest, his neck and head bent into his body. At last he fell into fitful, dream-bombarded sleep.

He was in his secret place in the pine grove, but a typhoon wind was blowing. The old tree in which he hid seemed unable to withstand the storm. Terrified, he huddled against the trunk while the wind crashed about him. The branch that covered his body cracked, then flew away, leaving him exposed. But, oh, wonderful, there before him stood his father, his arms outstretched! Over the warrior's green brocaded tunic he wore full armor—leather that had been dyed a deep lavender and stippled with gold and red. His horned helmet glittered, and the face below the helmet—the face. . . . Muna struggled to see the face, but it was as though his eyes blurred as he strove to see. But the voice. He knew the voice.

"The chrysanthemum tattoo, puppy. Why were you afraid to ask?"

And then, suddenly, he could see the face—a great purplish birthmark distorting it into an evil sneer. *"Har, har, har!"*

Muna cried out and awoke, struggling for breath. He looked around frightened, not knowing where he was; but as he moved, he felt the sword against his thigh. With a groan he remembered everything.

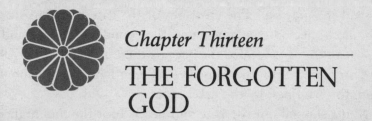

Chapter Thirteen

THE FORGOTTEN GOD

It was not yet dawn. Muna struggled to stand up, hampered by the sword as he tried to do so. His body was painfully stiff. He limped over to the communal well to wash.

The boy drew water and rinsed his face and hands. Then, remembering his filthy feet, he poured the remaining water over them. The cold splashed against them, sending a thrill of pain through his body. He thought of the bruises and cuts they had incurred the night before, and forgetting himself, stooped to examine them. But as he bent, the sword pressed tight against his trouser leg, and he quickly straightened. He could not risk tearing his trousers.

What should he do? He knew now that he could not conceal the sword on his body for long. He could not stoop or sit. He could scarcely lie down or get up with it bound to him. He would be found out. And what would happen to one who had stolen a sword with the name Fukuji engraved upon it? He looked above the roofs of the city to the surrounding mountains. Surely he could find a hiding place among their thick woods, a deserted temple, perhaps, or a shrine that pilgrims had forgotten.

Behind the eastern mountains the first streaks of red gashed the gray sky. The creatures of the gate began to stir. About the feet of the gate came the sounds of coughs and hoarse morning voices, as the beggars there shook themselves and stumbled into another day. At length the great doors were thrown open by the gatekeeper.

Muna slipped out the gate and headed for the mountains to the west of the capital. As he climbed a steep woodcutters' path into the mountain, the sheath of the sword first pressed against his thigh, then caught in his trouser seam, making the difficult climb all but impossible. He stopped and rebound the sword on the outside of his clothing before he continued his ascent.

He was not accustomed to such climbing. Often he had to grasp the trunks and roots of the pines growing along the pathway to pull himself upward. His breath cut through his throat and chest like a rusty blade. About halfway up he stopped, exhausted, and leaned against a sturdy maple.

"*He, he, he.*" At the sound of the laugh, Muna turned to meet an old wizened face. The man was bent under a load of firewood.

"Not used to climbing, are you?" The old eyes narrowed, and the lips parted to reveal a gaggle of decaying teeth.

With his hands on the sword hilt, Muna planted his feet as carefully as he could on the uneven ground.

"No, no." The wrinkled brown hand fluttered in protest. "Don't use me for your practice, ronin. *He, he, he.*" With that the old man bounded past him, taking the treacherous climb like a mountain goat. Muna could hear the giggle fade, as the woodcutter, with unbelievable speed, scampered up the path and out of sight.

Muna himself moved slowly upward, keeping his senses
rained for any indication of the old man. He dared not
eave the path, for he would have to be able to find his way
own again.

As he neared the summit, the path opened out onto a
ocky ledge. The boy turned to see below him the city, shim-

mering in the morning sun. He could make out at once the long complex of roofs that were the Imperial Palace, though as a commoner he had never been closer to the actual buildings than the stables. The glistening waters of the Kamo River flowed to the east. Across Gojo Bridge, antlike processions were moving to and from Rokuhara on the east bank. Sails of fishing boats and merchant vessels dotted the river.

He sought for other marks. Rashomon Gate to the south and the broad ribbon of Suzaku Oji moving north to the palace—the Gion Shrine. Not being religious, he could scarcely identify any of the larger temples by name. He strained for some sign that he could recognize in the southeast—but the tiny roofs of the artisans' shops huddled together under the smoke of their morning fires, and he could not distinguish one from another. He could almost smell the rice and bean soup—and the plum pickle.

Abruptly he headed for the summit. There was a tiny shrine there among the trees as he had hoped. A neglected one. The few paper prayers hanging on the nearby branches were brown and tattered. There was no food in the stone bowl before the god.

Cautiously the boy looked around. The meeting with the woodcutter had unnerved him. Birds were chirping noisily about like haggling street merchants, but there was no sign of a human presence.

"Old man?" he called loudly. "Hey, grandfather!" There was no answer but the flutter of wings and the annoyed squawks of the birds whose peace he had disturbed.

Quickly he stepped off twenty-five paces to the north of the shrine, sighting from the image of the god. There with a sharp stone he dug a trench about three feet deep and buried the sword. When he had covered it and stamped upon the place, he brought moss from deep within the woods to cover the scar. Then he scattered leaves and brush on top of the moss. No one could tell, he was sure; no one would be able to tell.

He half ran, half slid down the mountain, his heart lighter than it had been for weeks.

"*He, he, he.*"

Had he heard it or imagined it?

"*He, he, he.*"

Then the sound was lost in a chorus of chirpings and calls. It was only a bird. He was sure of it.

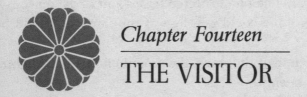

Chapter Fourteen

THE VISITOR

Fukuji lurched to a sitting position. It was not that a sound had awakened him but the lack of sound. No clanking of pots in the kitchen or *clop, clop* of clogs from the stones of the kitchen floor to those of the courtyard. No smell of steaming rice or hot bean soup in his nostrils.

The boy had overslept again. With a grunt the swordsmith slid out from beneath the quilts. Lately Muna had been up before him every morning. Well, it was too good to last. No. Not good. Strange.

The night shutters were still in place. Fukuji shoved, and they thundered aside, flooding the rooms with the summer sun.

"Muna!"

The bedding was empty. To the market for food, perhaps. Fukuji rolled up both sets of bedding and put them into the cupboard, then, down the stairs, slipping into the kitchen clogs at the foot.

The charcoal stove was there. At least the boy might have

started the fire before he left. The swordsmith picked up the stove. Once when Muna had begun the fire in the house, the fumes had nearly overcome them both. Fukuji slid open the door. The boy was learning, though today. . . .

His clog hit something soft as he stepped over the threshold. He caught his balance just in time, or he might have gone sprawling, stove and all, onto the cobblestones.

A straw sandal.

Slowly Fukuji put down the stove and reached for the sandal. His gaze jumped to the storehouse door. It seemed secure, but the swordsmith knew. By the gods, he had allowed himself to hope for better. But he knew. Only a thief goes in such haste that he forgets his sandals.

A chill went through his body though the sun was already high and hot. He had hoped. . . .

He laid the charcoal and made the fire, working methodically, not allowing his mind to stray from its narrow occupation. He filled his lungs and blew steadily until the charcoal caught fire, then fetched the fan and squatted before the low stove, fanning rhythmically, willing his mind to quietness.

When the noxious fumes had burned off, he carried the stove back into the kitchen, now keeping every nerve attendant to the sound of bubbling rice. Then, sitting stiffly on his feet upon the mat floor, he ate his meager breakfast of rice and pickle, chewing each bite with care. He rinsed his bowl and chopsticks in the water the boy had drawn the night before. Then carefully he swept out the house and kitchen.

He worked with great vigor, and by the time he went out to begin sweeping the courtyard, even his powerful shoulders would have ached if he'd allowed himself to notice anything other than the motion of the broom against the stones. *Whish, whish, whish.*

At the door of the forge he paused, but only for an instant; then he flung it aside.

"What an honor to meet you at last!"

The creature inside the room sat there cross-legged on the cover of the cold forge, a grin running like a long crack across his filthy beard.

Fukuji lowered the broom and steadied himself with it. It was not a devil. But what mortal would dare enter this place?

As if in answer, the ragged figure patted the forge. "As a bed, it lacks something in comfort."

"I dare say." Fukuji turned his back and started toward the house.

The devil, or whoever the stranger was, leaped nimbly from the forge and followed. "I haven't much time, but I'd be glad to stop long enough for a cup of tea or . . . ."

"No doubt." Without turning, Fukuji entered the kitchen door, the tall stranger at his heels.

They climbed into the mat room. Fukuji heard the man's clogs drop noisily upon the kitchen stones as the stranger brought his large dirty feet down on the clean matting of the room.

"The wine is cold," said the unwilling host.

The big hand went up in protest. "No need to warm it for me," his guest assured him.

The swordsmith brought a bottle and two tiny cups to the low table. Without looking up, he poured.

The man had his with a gulp, then smacked his lips appreciatively. "I have business with you, swordsmith."

Fukuji waited.

"You'll want to hear what I have to say."

Still Fukuji did not speak, so the man went on. "You know, of course, who stole the sword."

Still no answer.

"I know where he is. I'll get it back for you." He smiled and shook his massive head. "Oh, he's a little rascal, all right. You pity him, and *phew!*" He threw out his great hand. There was a ragged bandage on it. "But I'll get him for you" —he leaned forward—"and the sword."

Fukuji sat, not drinking, not moving, his narrow eyes set on the man before him. Of course, it was Muna's ronin, risen from pretended death.

The longer the swordsmith remained silent, the faster the ronin spoke, cursing the boy, and swearing by his own prowess in bringing the wicked to justice.

"All you have to do," he concluded, watching the swordsmith as carefully now as Fukuji watched him, "when I bring the boy in—with the sword—with the great sword, of course —is to give me one of your swords. Not a magnificent one such as that cur has stolen—just an ordinary"—he smiled as if to acknowledge the contradiction in his words—"an ordinary Fukuji sword." His eyes slid from the other's gaze to the bottle. "Shall we seal the bargain?"

"But you are mistaken." Fukuji's voice was even. "Nothing has been stolen." With that he got up and retrieved the visitor's clogs from the kitchen. Kneeling on the edge of the mat floor, he leaned down and placed them noiselessly on the stones of the entranceway. He remained there on his knees, waiting.

After a moment, the ronin stumbled to his feet and

stepped down, forcing the tattered thong of the clogs between his toes. In the narrow entranceway he turned and carefully measured the stiff form kneeling on the floor above.

"He was a knave, but in the end a clever one, eh?" The ronin paused, concentrating on loosening the dirt from under his left thumbnail with his right index finger. Then he nodded, lip thrust out. "An ancestry of rogues, but not a fool in the lot."

"Ancestry?" Fukuji echoed the word as though it had been wrenched from him. Then he cursed himself for his tone and made a conscious effort to bring his feelings into tight rein. "Ancestry?" he repeated tight-lipped.

Takanobu saw it and smiled. "You are steel, swordsmith. Tempered and polished—so polished. But"—he waved his finger toward the other's nose—"but I perceive a scratch." He drew his finger through the air. "A scratch!" he repeated, licking his chops over the word.

"Do you know the boy's father?" demanded the cold voice.

"Do I know the boy's father? *Har, har, har!*" He stopped abruptly and pointed at his own nose. "I! I am the luckless fellow!"

"You lie." Fukuji spat out the words.

The ronin squinted his eyes, not in anger, but simply to study his insulter. Slowly his head began to nod; then his fists began to beat his chest. At last he was jumping in a sort of crazy dance, his wooden clogs cracking down against the stones of the entranceway. Laughing, laughing, laughing.

The swordsmith watched in silence.

"You . . . you . . . ," Takanobu began to gasp out through his laughter. "You . . . who would believe? You . . . you're jealous of *me!*" And with that he fell back into his hysterical mirth, now clutching his belly as though the agony of the laughter might overcome him.

Fukuji waited, by the power of his will keeping every muscle of his body in check. At last, when the sounds were no more than hoarse gasps, the swordsmith spoke. "Show me the proof."

"What . . . ?" he was still struggling for breath. "What proof? The boy's a bastard. His mother's dead."

"But there was a tattoo. The boy told me. His mother had said he must look for it."

"A tattoo?"

"A small chrysanthemum on the right—no, left shoulder."

"A what?" The laughter was completely gone now.

"So. You lie."

"Yes. No." Confusion clouded the ronin's eyes and voice. "Master, I was only bluffing. . . ."

"So I thought."

"No, no. You don't understand." The wretched ronin pulled his tunic down off his left shoulder.

It was there. A tiny perfect flower.

At last Takanobu spit onto the stones. It broke the silence.

"You are a samurai," began the swordsmith.

"A ronin!" protested the man.

"A samurai. I expected you to bear full responsibility for your son's life and all his actions."

"Responsibility? Master, do you see me? Filthy, ragged— *swordless?* Have mercy." The words narrowed into a whine.

"Then if you do not intend to act as a father. . . ."

"I give him to you!" Takanobu threw both hands into the air. "Every hair on his cursed head. I'll never come near him again. I swear, I swear." He slapped his hands to his chest. "Just leave *me* alone."

"My pleasure," the swordsmith replied drily.

"Besides"—the old bravado began to seep back—"there must be thousands of tattoos like this."

"Quite possibly."

"You know how these fool artists are. 'For *you* something special!' " He pursed his lips in imitation. "Special! *Pfft.*" He spat on the stones again.

"Yes, well. . . ."

"A good morning to you, sir." He ducked his head. "No hard feelings, eh? I don't touch him. You don't mention me to the authorities. Agreed?"

So the rogue was in trouble with the authorities. Good. It would serve as the club he needed to keep the ronin at a distance.

Fukuji gave a nod that was both agreement and dismissal. When the clackety-clack of clogs in flight could no longer be heard, he brought water and scrubbed the stones of the entranceway.

Chapter Fifteen

DEATH OF DREAMS

There was a rage pounding in his head. Not since he had seen his young wife lying dead beside the body of their still-born son had Fukuji known such a rage. The ronin would have marveled at the transformation—the steel-cold man in the white heat of madness.

He made a roaring fire within the forge. The reflected flames burned like the furnaces of hell in his eyes as he plunged the strip of metal into the fire. He was naked to the waist, and the sweat rolled in streams from his shoulders. With the tongs he took the glowing metal to the anvil and brought the giant hammer upon it. *Clang! Clang! Clang!* And with every clang, a voice broke out in an agonized shout, "Yah! Yah! Yah!" as though the metal itself cried out.

At last, rage spent, he cast the tortured steel into the rubbish and extinguished the fire. He drew water from the well and poured it over his head and body. When he had dressed himself, he fell upon the mat floor in exhausted sleep.

"Fukuji?"

He was awake at once, but it was not the boy. Muratani of

the Heike had come. The boy's message had been a strange one. Was all well with the master?

"The boy has left my service."

"And the sword?"

"Ah, the sword. . . ."

"Shall I look for him, Fukuji? Has he done you injury?"

"No, no. It is a private affair. I will look for him myself."

For a while, neither spoke. Then the samurai said gently, "How may I serve you, uncle?"

The older man looked up, startled by Muratani's warm language. No one called him uncle. His manner forbade the common familiarities of speech. But now the samurai's kind tone comforted him.

"The boy has a father—somewhere. . . ."

"And?"

"And it may be that Lord Kiyomori could find him."

"But you and Lord Kiyomori are not on cordial terms."

"How do you know that?"

The samurai laughed. "A swordsmith who refused to make a sword for the Emperor's highest-ranking officer will not, in any case, fail to make news. Let me speak a word in your behalf, sir. It could do no harm."

"I would be grateful for that."

Within the day the word came that Lord Kiyomori would welcome the swordsmith at his Rokuhara mansion. Always meticulous, Fukuji bathed and dressed the following morning with even more than his usual care, and refusing Muratani's offer of a sedan chair, walked across Gojo Bridge and presented himself at Rokuhara well before noon.

"Ah, Fukuji—" Lord Kiyomori waved him to a cushion

near his own. "How long has it been? Two years now?"

Fukuji nodded in reply. He had always liked Kiyomori, for the general was a true man, unlike most of the soft-skinned aristocrats that pranced about the Emperor.

Wine was brought, and as they drank, Kiyomori talked in his rough unpolished manner—of the summer weather, of his elder son's slow progress in his swordfighting lessons. He spoke, too, of his father and his desire to make a pilgrimage in the dead man's honor.

Fukuji had listened to the general's ramblings, alert for an opening. This seemed to be it. "Your father was a great and good man, my lord."

"Always."

"How fortunate you were to have had such a father."

"Yes." Both men knew what everyone in the capital knew —that when Tadamori of the Heike had married the courtesan known as the Lady of Gion, he had taken her bastard son and raised him as his own. But the bond between father and son had been such that only a fool brought up the question of blood ties. And that fool only once.

"My Lord Kiyomori—the favor I come to beg. . . ."

"Yes, your favor, swordsmith!"

"It concerns a boy who. . . ." He paused. "Actually, I need information. . . ."

The general chuckled. "You've come to the wrong place. Rumors reach me last of all. Ask any of my retainers."

"No, this concerns a man, a samurai, who bears a tattoo— a tiny chrysanthemum tattoo on his left shoulder. Do you know such a man?"

"I should think so," Kiyomori said heartily. "There were about two hundred of us at the beginning. . . ."

"Two hundred?"

"At the beginning. It was a youthful stunt. After one of the voyages to the Inland Sea, when my father took me pirate-chasing, a group of us took it into our heads to honor our great victories with a suitable tattoo." He refilled both cups. "I'm told it started quite a rage for chrysanthemum tattoos at the time. Some of which"—he wiped his mouth on his sleeve, and above the brocade his eyes twinkled—"some of which were obviously regretted later. Fashions in politics being what they are, and tattoos, alas. . . ." He spread his hands in mock dismay.

"I see. Quite hopeless then."

"Well, surely your samurai has some sort of body upon which this tattoo of his is affixed? Come now, you must tell me what else you know of him besides his wretched little chrysanthemum." And the general pressed the swordsmith until at last Fukuji told him all he knew about the boy, except that he had stolen a sword.

"I fear for the child, alone and without friends or money, in our troubled city. I do not know to what end this search of his may lead him." He dropped his gaze, aware that Kiyomori was studying him as he spoke.

"Ah, my poor Fukuji," he said in a voice usually reserved for women, "if you so crave a son, why do you not marry again?"

"I desire no son," he replied and knew only as he heard his own words that he lied.

"I have ways of finding people," the general said quietly. "I could find the boy within hours, and it is not impossible that I might find his father as well if that is what you desire. Tell me when the boy was born. We have records of who goes to Awa and for what official purposes. No one can be trusted as you know."

"I should be grateful."

"Grateful enough"—and Fukuji looked up to see why the general hesitated—"grateful enough to change your mind?" He took a long sip of wine and waited.

"Forgive me, my lord. I was wrong to come. I cannot make you a sword."

"No?" The voice was not angry.

"Your feud with Yoshitomo of the Genji hangs over the city like a giant millstone on a thread. Should I hand you a sword to cut that thread?"

"Fukuji, you are a swordmaker, not a child." The general rose and began to stride back and forth. "What do you imagine men do with swords? Hang them in their sashes for decorations?"

"I know what some men do with swords."

"Oh, it is easy for you to posture righteousness, Fukuji." Kiyomori hurled about to face him. "My uncle was a traitor. Do you think I wished to kill him? Would I be more worthy in your eyes if I had stood aside like a bawling woman and ordered his death at another's hand?"

"I cannot judge such matters, sir."

"Oh, but you *do* judge, Fukuji. You make the instruments of death and then judge the men that use them. Bah! Do you know you are a hypocrite, swordsmith? A hypocrite?"

"Yes," Fukuji replied. "I know."

He bowed toward the general's angry back and left the room without waiting to be dismissed.

Fukuji began his search in the marketplace near his shop. He walked slowly, casually nodding at acquaintances, but then he would hear a word or a laugh that would jerk his head toward its source. But it was never the face he looked for. By dusk he had worked his way through the streets of the artisans and the bawdy district until before him loomed the great ghostly bulk of Rashomon whose towers some said held the rotting flesh of the outcast dead and under whose shadow crept the scum of the living.

He walked slowly from booth to booth, buying nothing, speaking to no one, not really looking at those things his eyes seemed to be examining. For all his senses were straining for evidence of the boy's whereabouts.

And then he saw him. He was huddled against a pillar as though he was freezing, though the evening air was hot and humid.

Fukuji stepped into the shadow of a booth. What should he say? How could he approach the boy? Muna would think he had come for vengeance. Better not to speak until Muna could see his face and know that he did not come in anger. He began to move toward the portico.

The boy jumped to his feet. Fukuji could see that he was quivering.

"Muna!" he shouted. But the boy ran into the darkness of the portico.

He might have found him. The boy more than likely had darted into one of the openings in the tower. He might even now be gazing out at him. But he forced himself to turn around. He had been a fool to come. A fool to go to Rokuhara. A fool to think he could find the boy or that he should. Muna was not some metal the swordsmith could pound to his own design. He was nearly a man. He must find his own way.

It was a long time before Muna's body, pressed against the damp stones of the tower wall, ceased to shake. In the blackness he listened for the sound of Fukuji's step. He listened so intently that he heard it, beyond any doubt, five or six times, only to have it come to nothing.

Gradually the fear that he was caught turned to a more terrible kind of fear—the fear that he was not to be caught at all. He was a thief and a traitor; he deserved his punishment; but for some perverse reason, known only to that strange, inscrutable man, he was not to be given it.

Fukuji would go home and take out his zither and sing a sad song that would explain it all, but no one would be there to hear it. "We are dead to each other, I suppose," thought Muna. "And all that ever bound us is buried on the mountain."

He tried to be glad, for he was free now. He had no obligations that anyone wished him to repay. He should feel relief, but *ara!* all he felt was a great black emptiness. It even had an odor, this feeling—strongly sweet, laced to memory of plague and typhoon. It stung in his nostrils, invading his throat and belly. He thrashed his arms about in the darkness, struggling to find the opening through which he had entered. He stumbled and his left hand fell into a mass of—a horse's mane? What insanity? Too soft for a horse. No. What hell had he fallen into? But there was no question. He recognized the smell now. He snatched up his hand, stumbling across the—whatever lay there—and clawed at the walls until he found the slit.

To the well he ran as though all the rotting ghouls of the nether world were at his heels, but wash as he might, the odor clung.

He dreamed that night. The great warrior in his gold-horned helmet came again, holding out his arms. And Muna ran to them with all his might. "Father! Father!" he cried with joy, but the face that looked down into his own was a grinning skull.

Chapter Sixteen

THE SWORD OF FUKUJI

At first he felt himself a peculiar creature among all the peculiar creatures of the gate. His clothes were better than anyone else's, while at the same time he was barefoot.

He caught the beggars staring at him. Their eyes went from his face to his clothes to his feet and back to his face. Their expressions never changed, but Muna could feel the questions behind those blank eyes.

In the early days he went out beyond the gate into the mountains when he craved privacy. There was none at the gate, of course. There by a stream he would take off his clothes and wash them and himself. He always returned to the gate. He had sentenced himself to hell, and he did not try to escape.

But before the summer was over, the weather had begun to fade his clothes. He had lost the cloth that bound his long hair, and it hung tangled about his shoulders. Gradually he ceased trying to groom it, or to keep his clothes or body clean. And, without realizing it, Muna melted into the hodgepodge of his surroundings and became a true creature of the gate, no more to be noticed or remarked upon than one more fly on a pile of manure.

The summer chilled into fall. Above the city the maples lit the mountains like a rash of tiny fires among the pines. The sky was like a brilliant jewel that the sun-goddess Amaterasu had washed with sparkling rain and rubbed to shining with the hem of her trailing garment.

But there was a dullness in the boy. The filth, the restless nights, the grubbing for food, he had forgotten to hate them now. Occasionally he would look down at his feet and realize all over again that they were bare. It always seemed to come as a surprise. He should have spent his few coins for sandals, he would tell himself all over again. The food was gone so quickly. Soon it would be winter, and he would still be barefoot.

When winter came, renewed rumblings of revolt came with it. There had been mysterious fires during the fall and open squabbling between Genji and Heike in the streets, but by the last month of the year even the creatures of the gate were laying odds as to when open warfare would break out and which clan would triumph. And even in his dullness Muna knew that Takanobu would be among the rebels.

But across the Kamo River in the great mansion at Rokuhara, Lord Kiyomori seemed deaf to rumor and blind to the violence in the streets. He had planned a pilgrimage to Kumano Shrine in honor of his dead father, and he was determined to make the trip before the beginning of the New Year.

When he was nearly a week's journey from the capital, the

Genji struck. They put the Emperor under heavy guard and seized all the positions of authority. Genji soldiers were posted all over the city, and preparations were made to capture Rokuhara itself. But news of the coup d'état reached Lord Kiyomori, and he gathered armies from the outlying provinces and marched toward the capital.

There were always soldiers about Rashomon, for at the gate the girls were cheaper than the ones on Rokujo Avenue, and there were plenty of pawnbrokers who never asked questions. But now there was an ugly mood in the Genji troops who were sent to patrol the gate. They were arrogant in their swift capture of the city, but at the same time, they dreaded the return of Kiyomori with his army athirst for revenge. So they badgered the creatures of the gate. They pushed them away from their own bonfires and took goods and girls without payment. They were coarse men to begin with, and their fears of what lay outside the gate made them even louder and more brutish.

Muna did not object. He now belonged fully to that class of people who expect to be bullied by the rest of the world, who think that by objecting they will only bring further misery upon themselves. He had no dreams of personal worth left to smash.

Then one day he saw the woodcutter. He was talking to one of the Genji warriors. "*He, he, he.*" Muna could hear that horrible pinched laugh, but he could not make out any of the conversation.

Suppose the old man had seen him hide the sword? Suppose he was, even now, contriving to sell the sword of Fukuji to one of these brutish guards? A vision of Fukuji holding the shining blade up to the sun flashed across Muna's mind.

That sword at the side of one of these disgusting beasts?

He hurried through the gate. His feet, wrapped in rags against the winter, could scarcely make their way up the icy path. He clawed his way up, from tree to tree, snatching at roots and dried foliage that often gave way, so that he fell backward and had to scratch his way up again.

Like a frog in a well—a frog in a well. But he clung on with teeth and hands and cruelly frostbitten feet, until at last he gained the summit and came to the neglected shrine with the empty food cup.

For months now he had forgotten every human feeling, except hunger, but now fear loomed up greater than even hunger, sending its clawing tentacles through every limb of his ravaged body. He paced off the twenty-five steps from the idol's head.

Was the place disturbed? Yes. No. How could he tell? He tried to dig through the frozen earth with his bare fingers, but he soon had to give this up. He found a sharp stick that broke at once with a brittle snap. At last he found a pointed rock and began hacking away at the ground. "*Augh, augh.*" He stopped to listen, but the strange noise he heard was his own breath coming out in sobs.

Three feet into the frozen ground. It seemed an eternity. But at last he saw a glitter—one of the gold-leafed chrysanthemums on the sheath. The gods—whom he had long forgotten—the gods be praised.

He continued digging until the whole length of the sword appeared. He lifted it gently, and taking the hem of his tunic, wiped the dirt from the hilt, the filigreed guard, and the gold-leaf chrysanthemum flowers on the sheath.

Then, almost reverently, he withdrew the blade. It was

spotless. The engraved characters "Fukuji" blinked up as if to mock him. Quickly he resheathed the sword and bound it once more under his trousers.

As he passed the shrine, he wished he had something—a rice cake, a piece of fish—but having nothing, he broke off a bit of pine and placed it in the empty offering cup.

So it was that night that Muna stood by the communal fire with the sword of Fukuji bound to his side.

At first the soldier simply came up beside Muna as the boy sought to warm himself. But then a second soldier came up for whom there was no place in the circle.

"Hey, stiff leg! Make way for your protector!"

Not knowing who "stiff leg" might be, Muna simply glanced about the circle in the stupid manner of a beggar boy.

"I mean you, stiff leg!" With that the soldier gave him a tremendous kick that sent Muna tumbling over toward the fire. With a terrible rip, the sword tore its way out of the now-ragged garment, and for a few seconds the gold figures on the sheath glinted in the firelight.

Muna struggled to his feet, pulling the shreds of his trouser leg together in an attempt to cover the sword, but it was useless. Everyone had seen it.

"*He, he, he*. So that's where you had it hidden!" From nowhere the old woodcutter appeared, jumping up and down with glee. "I combed the mountain, I did! And it was in his trousers all the time. *He, he, he*."

The soldier pushed the old man aside. "Let's see it, boy. What do you have there?"

Muna backed away and then darted through the circle of startled creatures surrounding the bonfire. He ran up the steps of the gate, but the great doors were closed. He turned to find both soldiers just below him. They stood with their swords drawn.

"Either you are a spy or a thief. Which?"

Muna stood cornered like some dumb, uncomprehending animal.

"It doesn't really matter. You will die for either crime. But if you give us the sword, we might . . . ."

The sword. This cruel lout thought he could wear the sword of Fukuji? Something human, some ancient memory of cleansing fire and pure water, stirred in Muna's brain.

"Come on, now. Give it to me." *Like a good puppy*.

The boy's hand went down into the fold of his tunic. Slowly, carefully, he drew out the shining blade.

"That's right . . . ."

"*Ararrrr!*" Like a tiger he sprang upon them. They fell back in startled confusion from the deadly path of the blade. And the boy ran, his matted hair streaming behind him like a madman, through the streets of the city, the sword high in his hand. He was taking it home.

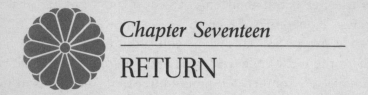

Chapter Seventeen
RETURN

The day has ended
And the visitors have left—
In the mountain village
All that remains is the howl
Of the storm winds from the peak.

A tiny oil lamp flickered at his side, throwing moving shadows against the wall of swords. Fukuji sat close to the charcoal brazier, strumming his zither and singing softly. The cold was intense, and he stopped often to warm his numb fingers against the sides of the pottery brazier. Tonight all the songs seemed to be melancholy ones, for the storm winds were howling about the wintry city. No one could protect her from the devastation they would bring. He struck a line of savage chords, which melted at last into another lonely air of the provinces.

I passed by the beach
At Tago and saw
The snow falling, pure and white,
High on the peak of Fuji.

And his spirit quieted as in his mind's eye the sacred mountain rose from the plains in her symmetrical perfection. Perfect, that is, except for the crater at her summit—her scar which testified to the tumult that once had raged within her. Was she not the more beautiful for her imperfection?

"Fukuji?"

A caller at this hour? The swordsmith put down the zither and carried the lamp to the front entryway.

It was a strange sight that met his startled eyes. A beggar or ragpicker with filthy garments and long, matted hair stood barefoot on the stones.

But he was holding out a sword.

"Fukuji. I have brought back the sword."

Then the swordsmith knew him. It was Muna.

Speechless, the man took the sword.

From his shredded tunic the boy took the sheath, and placing this at Fukuji's feet, he turned to go.

"Wait." The man found his voice at last. "Where are you going?"

The boy turned around. His eyes had gone dull again.

Fukuji knelt, bringing his own face level with the boy's. "You can't go back into the streets. Kiyomori has an army assembled on the banks of the Kamo. By morning the city will flow with blood." He put down the lamp and busied himself, resheathing the sword. "Stay awhile with me here."

He could see confusion in the boy's eyes now and a refusal coming to the dry lips. But the swordsmith put his powerful hand on the boy's arm and helped him into the house.

Chapter Eighteen

SONG OF THE SMALL HILLS

That night, as Fukuji had foretold, the storm of war broke over the Capital of Eternal Peace. By morning the streets ran with the blood of Genji and Heike, mingled in death. Before the week was out, fires raged uncontrolled in every district, and terror stalked avenue and alley as the victorious Heike routed Genji sympathizers from their hiding places and left their bodies unburied in the street.

By dawn of the first day the swordsmith was in the street, searching out the homeless wounded. He and the boy slept on the stones of the kitchen floor, when they slept, for the upper rooms of the shop were crowded with pallets on which lay the injured and dying. Fukuji and Muna moved among them, giving them water and tiny rations of food. Thus they passed both the birthday of the boy and the opening of the New Year.

When Kiyomori regained the city, Yoshitomo and his Genji retainers tried to flee, but they were tracked down, caught, and beheaded on the banks of the Kamo. For years afterward, the boy could not pass the gory execution grounds without a shudder. He hoped that Takanobu had escaped, because for all his perfidy, the ronin had once been his friend. Nor was the man really a traitor. He had cared nothing for emperor or clan. His only allegiance had been to his own roguish skin.

By the time the plum tree had defied the wintry air with its first pale blossoms, the city had returned to a kind of normalcy with order enforced by the presence of Heike guards. The patients in the shop who had not died could now be returned to the shacks thrown up over the ruins of their former houses. Then the green promise of the willows on Suzaku Oji was met once more with the profusion of cherry blossoms. And seeing the faithfulness of nature, the people of the city took heart and began to rebuild.

Muna found himself once more at his old tasks—his woman's work of sweeping and scrubbing and cooking—but now he did them all with a kind of fierce joy, known only to those who have escaped the jaws of Hell.

Fukuji was pleased with him. The swordsmith did not have to say so. When he emerged from the forge, his eyes

would pass across the immaculate courtyard, and he would nod. Over his bowl of rice his sharp eyes would relax. "Umph," he would grunt. It was reward enough.

Then one night he stopped his chopsticks in midair, the rice halfway to his mouth. "*Ara!*" he exclaimed. "I forgot. At the New Year you became a man—during the troubles it slipped past me."

"*Mmmm.*" The boy nodded. He was pleased. Why should Fukuji concern himself at all?

"You'll be wanting a proper name, now that you're of age." It was half a question, half a statement of fact. "Have you chosen one?"

The boy shook his head. "I don't have any experience in such things," he mumbled shyly. "Perhaps you . . . ."

"No, no." The swordsmith waved his chopsticks. "You must choose. It is your name, and it must please only you."

Muna had thought about it, of course. At one time it had been almost an obsession, the name that would replace "No Name" once and for all. But he had not thought of it now

for a long time. It belonged to his daydream world of many months before, before Takanobu had reappeared and Kawaki had died. Before he had let go of his phantom of a father. Before he knew what happened to beautiful girls who were orphaned. Before he knew that he himself could lie and steal and betray. For several days he thought again about his name—the one he would carry and give to his children. He took out and examined again all the grand names he had once considered, but now they seemed pompous and unsuitable. He was what he was. No other name would change that.

On a night in late spring, the two of them sat in the courtyard while Fukuji played his zither and sang Isonokami's "Song of the Small Hills."

> How march the four seasons in succession
> Unwaywardly, for the eons past!
> Grasses that greet the spring in flowered tapestry;
> The summer trees curtained in leaves;
> In the sad breath of autumn, the falling fruit;
> Bare branches before the shrill winter wind—
> When I see these seasonal things I know
> How man too must flourish and die.

The clear tenor of the swordsmith's voice shimmered in the night air—the voice bright above the zither's chords like raindrops on a spider web.

> Of the hills of Paradise have I heard
>   but never seen;
> Toward the land of the gods I gaze,
>   knowing not the way.
> I know only that to make a mountain

You must pile the little clods one by one.
Where then should I seek nobility?
In what delights the heart there is nothing mean.

Muna recalled the day of his mother's burial. He had
climbed the hill and looked down upon the land of his native island. Had he despised what he had seen? No. But he
had lusted for the nobility that he thought was his beyond
the sea.

And these ragged hills
That shut not out the coursing sun;
This clear bright pond
Ruffled in the wind;
Pines that nod from their crag in greeting;
Rocks shining from the river bottom
  beneath drifting watery mirrors;
Scattered clouds that cloak the summits
  in shadows;
The half-risen moon which lights the vales,
When from tree to tree dart crying birds.

Muna recalled those two other climbs. The little, forgotten
god of the hill who had saved the sword—had saved him.

To these will I abandon, will I entrust my life,
The Great Creator, in the variety of his works,
Blesses as well the lowly and the small.
When all philosophy I resolve in this one act,
I may stride the leviathan seas and they
  will not hold me:
Into the dark heart of all being I shall ride
And dwell in the spacious halls of the ant.

"Blesses as well the lowly and the small." If only his Little Mother had known and taught him this. But, no, he would not have listened. He had longed so for a name to prove his own nobility. Muna sat silent long after the strings had ceased trembling under the stroke of the final chord. The man waited.

"It may seem strange to you, sir," the boy said at last. "But I have decided to keep the name of Muna."

The grizzled head bowed over the zither, striking from it chords that seared the boy's body like flames, leaping and dancing. Not angry fire, devouring the innocent like a roaring dragon, but powerful, cleansing, joyful fire. Then abruptly the music was over. Fukuji stood up and carried the zither into the storehouse. When he came out, he was holding the chrysanthemum sheathed sword that Muna had stolen so many months before.

He walked quickly toward the boy, unsheathing the sword as he came. Fukuji dropped the sheath on his stool. He reached out his great left hand and grasped the boy's hair where it was bound at the back of the neck. His right hand raised the sword. Muna was too startled to move or cry out. Then, *slash*, the sharp blade cut through the band of cloth. Fukuji handed the long hank of hair to the boy.

"It would be dangerous to enter the forge trailing this," he said. Then he smiled.

In this way, Muna of Awa became apprenticed to Fukuji of Nagano, master swordsmith of the capital. And the sword of Fukuji, which had been bound to Muna's side, now hung on the sword wall unsheathed, so that any who entered the shop could read the motto engraved upon it:

"Through fire is the spirit forged."